"A sharp look at political deconstruction and the realities of revolution, *One Last Game* presents a unique, yet chillingly plausible future. Fast-paced, heartfelt, and unexpectedly hopeful."

— J.S. DEWES
author of *The Last Watch*

"A clever and chilling high-stakes novella that asks what freedom we're willing to give up in exchange for peace and stability."

— CLAIRE BARNER
author of *Moonrising*

"With gripping prose and a cast of memorable characters, T.A Chan spins an ever so relevant story about the dangers of eco-fascism and the cost of revolution, reminding us once again that broken systems thrive on complacency."

— FRANCESCA TACCHI
author of *Let the Mountains Be My Grave*

"*One Last Game* is a brutal ride of a novella. With one of the most innovative dystopia mechanics I've ever read, Chan delivers a *Hunger Games*-esque narrative that still manages to leave the reader with a droplet of hope."

— A.D. SUI
author of *The Dragonfly Gambit*

ONE LAST GAME

ONE LAST GAME

T.A. CHAN

FAIRWOOD PRESS
Bonney Lake, WA

ONE LAST GAME

A Fairwood Press Book
September 2025
Copyright © 2025 T.A. Chan
All Rights Reserved

First Edition

Fairwood Press
21528 104th Street Court East
Bonney Lake, WA 98391
www.fairwoodpress.com

Cover character art © Yara Ridanti
Game board interior image © Tom Canty
Cover and book design by Patrick Swenson

ISBN: 978-1-958880-34-0

First Fairwood Press Edition: September 2025

Printed in the United States of America

For those who sustain hope for a better future.

A note to readers: For a list of trigger warnings,
please see www.authortachan.com

CHAPTER 1
NIKO

NIKO BREEZED THROUGH THE PRE-GAME check-in with perfunctory rote. Paxania Stadium was his second home. Located on the neutral grounds of the International Conflict Resolution Court, the iconic stadium was where all the Battle Games *and* International Peacetime Games were played, an irony that wasn't lost on Niko. He'd stood in the center of the arena dozens of times. Sometimes representing the Atlantic Archipelago Nation as a war-time conqueror, other times as peacetime ambassador—but always a victor.

Today's Game: Atlantic Archipelago Nation vs Antarctican Republic for control over shipping routes. After two years bickering over tables and unable to reach a satisfactory resolution, both countries voted to resolve the issue with a Battle Game.

Sweat pearled against Niko's hairline as the spotlight blazed down on him. The large, red digits on the clock indicated the game had ticked over an hour—and the victory was finally within sight. event. Two more moves and a win, then he would match the number of Battle Games won by the legendary Coach Ivonna. A record that had stood for decades, and a feat that earned her retirement from Player to a position as Coach.

Niko leaned forward in his chair, mind utterly calm and focused on the Game. Nothing in the world existed except for the gameboard and his opponent. The two of them were on the gaming platform, a stage floating a dozen meters midair. Drones zipped overhead like vultures and broadcasted the Players onto giant screens standing sentinel around the stadium. Gamecasters commented on each move made over the arena speakers.

With practiced poise, Niko scanned the Set board and game pieces arranged on the table. The board was a lovely slab of polished rosewood with gridded lines burned into it, straight as soldiers in formation. Small black and white stones had been placed on the intersection points. Niko plucked a black stone from his bowl and placed it on B4. He raised his chin at the other Player.

Your move.

Judson represented the Antarctican Republic, a relatively peaceful nation that rarely got get involved with international conflicts. And it showed in Judson's game play. He didn't play with the savage edge Niko employed. He didn't walk that fine line between *vicious cleverness* and *dirty cheating* that Niko danced upon.

Sweat dotted Judson's hairline as he plopped his own stone down. A futile attempt to salvage some lost grids.

Niko's heartbeat pulsed in the back of his throat as he laid the winning stone down on the board and the audience roared with approval.

GAME OVER flashed in bright purple on the display screens. It was the color of the uniform Niko wore. In the sold-out stands reaching toward the blushing sunset sky, the maroon-clad crowd cheered, screaming their win—Niko's win, a collective win—in a war cry while gold and mauve confetti showered down like ash.

A lone curl of paper stuck to his cheek, the texture rough and unexpected, yanking Niko out of his detached headspace and grounding him in the moment. He swiped the piece of gold confetti off as the roar of spectators chanting his catchphrase "Control the board! Control the board!" filled his ears. He clenched his hand, fingers pressing the confetti into his sweat dampened palm.

And finally—*finally*, he allowed himself to feel the emotions he'd been keeping on mute. He'd won. *He'd won.* A heady blend of fear-hope-relief coursed through his bloodstream and lit up his nerves.

Niko jumped up in a bout of exhilaration, sweeping the stones off the Set board. Fallen soldiers on a battlefield. He spun, arms raised, a gleaming smile slashed across his face as his fingers split into a V. He'd secured both a victory for his country and a prize of 2 million credits. In theory, he had every right to savor the win.

In reality, he hated how the thrill of triumph both delighted the competitive streak in his core and sickened him at the same time.

Niko's stomach knotted as he forced the smile to stay on his face. *I can't do this anymore.*

Stairs unfolded from beneath the gaming platform, allowing access from the stadium floor.

Judson stared down at the scattered stones with his jaw clenched, matching the subdued mood of the Antarctican citizens. His jaw clenched tighter still when Referee guards marched up the stairs and surrounded him.

The guards held their rifles at the ready even though Judson gave no indication of fleeing.

Not yet, anyway. They usually didn't run until later, when the cost of their loss became a visceral, apparent affair.

The jumbo screens flickered, and the pixels changed. Half of the displays depicted drone footage of Archipelago citizens flooding the streets in jubilant celebration. The national flag—an aquamarine backdrop studded with a yellow sun surrounded by stars—fluttered from balconies, silent fireworks peppered the sky, and biodegradable paint sloshed across buildings and streets.

On the other half of the screens, a map of the Antarctican Republic materialized like morning mist. A grid overlaid the map, reminiscent of the game board Niko and Judson had fought over. One of the gridded squares on the map blinked, turning orange, before randomly jumping around the digital lattice and highlighting different squares in a frenzied dance. A1, B4, H17, C3. Three-hundred and twenty-four squares in total. The Antarctican Republic was a small country— the larger ones had thousands of squares.

The stadium shushed now, enraptured by the hypnotizing flash of the orange square hopping from space to space. Gamblers watching a slot machine spin, spin, spin. A countdown ticked in the upper right-hand corner.

7 . . . 6 . . . 5 . . .

The silence pulled taut. Even Niko lowered his arms in morbid interest and respect.

. . . 4 . . .

Judson stoically stared at the screen, his mouth twitching as he muttered the same phrase under his breath over and over. Later, people would say he was chanting *G3, G4, H1, H2.* The squares corresponding with the ones located over the ocean on the gridded map.

"THREE," the purple crowd screamed.

The Referees white-knuckled their rifles.

"TWO . . . ONE!"

The orange square ended its frantic dance, pulsing over B5.

Judson briefly closed his eyes when the stats of B5 glowed onto the screens.

Location: B5
Area: 1,000 square kilometers (833 land, 167 water)
Population: Approx. 62,000

The drone footage switched once more, cutting to various views of B5. To the panicking citizens inhabiting that unlucky spot.

Bile stung the roof of Niko's mouth. *Better them than us,* he reassured himself. *At least it's not us.*

A new countdown appeared on the screens: 10 minutes.

On livestream, angry Antarcticans threw rocks at the drones, but they all fell short and the drones continued observing the pandemonium below like a hawk watching a hare. Even the Archipelago citizens toned

back their celebrating to stare at the footage of Antarcticans rushing to vacate B5. The roads clogged with
refugees—some in solar cars, others by bike, and still
others by foot. Those near the border hurried toward
neighboring squares for escape. The ones who weren't
so lucky turned to the shelters. The bunkers wouldn't
fit everyone, of course, but some were better than none.

5 minutes left.

Judson pushed to his feet, eyes glittering beneath
the dying sunset. The Referees stepped closer, shrinking
their circle around him. Still, Judson didn't flinch nor
show any signs of anger or despair.

Perhaps he knew his face was being broadcasted
across the world, and refused viewers the satisfaction
of witnessing his breakdown.

Perhaps he had already accepted his fate.

Either way, Niko's chest hitched with sympathy.
Did that make him a traitor to the Archipelago, that he
empathized with the enemy? He didn't know, didn't care
anymore. *Better them than us.* Maybe if he repeated it
enough, the words would carry more conviction.

1 minute left on the clock.

The Referees primed their shock rifles, the electric
buzz permeating the air.

30 seconds.

Two guards wearing thick, rubber gloves gripped
Judson by the arms and neck, holding him in place.

10 seconds.

Some might call the juxtaposition of the scene unfolding in square B5 poetic, or surreal. The manicured
grass interspersed with native flowers and lush sculpted
forests a contrast to the gray mob surging down the

roads; the grazing deer and sleeping foxes unbothered by the car honks. Urban wildlife had coexisted with humans for generations, and no longer feared the filthy chaos that came with civilization.

0 seconds.

A pause that froze for eternity—until it didn't.

A Referee flicked the safety off their rifle and strode up to Judson. The muzzle pressed against his chest, and then the trigger was pulled. Thirty amps coursed through Judson's heart. His eyes rolled back, his muscles spasmed, grasping at its final seconds of life. And then he slumped when the trigger was released.

Niko dragged his eyes away from Judson's body and stared up at the screen straight ahead. His gaze was unseeing as he mentally replayed the utter peace that had rolled across Judson's face right before he died. And if Niko felt a shred of envy that Judson had finally escaped the life of a Player, that must've been his imagination.

Niko blinked and focused back to the present, just in time to see his final mark of victory.

On the towering screens, the first tendrils of the killing fog rolled through the streets of B5 before the display cut to black.

CHAPTER 2

IMANI

THE FOG'S NAME WAS KARLO.

Imani watched the pink mist drift across the tiny screen stuck to the back of the driver's headrest in the Custodian van.

She didn't know exactly where the name *Karlo* stemmed from, but according to Kit, the name was derived from some personified weather phenomena that frequented the Western Pacific Bay—previously known as *San Francisco,* a peninsula that'd sunk underwater. One of the early casualties of global warming, before the billionaires of the world finally realized their best chance of survival was restoring Earth to its more natural, primitive state. Isolated bunkers, rocketing off to Mars, and doomsday homesteads were only short-term solutions. (Imani could attest the latter was a terrible idea.)

Thus, the Great Restoration of 2065 began in the name of saving both planet and civilized society: an ambitious project that saw the rise and fall of countries and alliances, inspired successful eco-cities on a large scale, and ushered in the first iteration of the Battle Games.

The initial games back in 2078 looked very different from the matches Imani now cleaned up after. She plucked at the seatbelt across her chest, antsy to leave after four hours on the solar cell road. The confines of the vehicle cabin reminded her of hiding in the pantry, knees shaking, eyes squeezed shut, hands clasped over her ears while gunshots and shrieks echoed throughout the compound—

"Bah, Judson shouldn't have given up his corner space for three extra stones." Oran's comment cemented Imani back in the present. The rear of the van comprised of two benches stretching the length of the walls, facing each other. Currently, three Custodians (Oran, Kit, and Imani) occupied the back while the team lead remained in the driver's seat, despite the steering being on autopilot (regulation requirement). "At the hour and thirteen minute mark, Judson played Dirkin's Corner," Oran continued loftily. "Such a neophyte mistake to make. Judson should've known better, considering he's been training his whole life."

Imani arched a brow at Oran's hotshot attitude. Seriously, where do people get the confidence to believe they would play a better Game than a highly trained Player? She kicked her feet up to the other bench, nudging Kit in the thigh. "If Judson's been playing Set since he could hold a stone, chances are he *didn't* make a mistake."

Each year, children between the ages of four and eight were screened (that is, children who weren't secluded from society by a delusional cult), and those with an aptitude for strategy games were whisked away to be trained by the nation's top coaches to excel in ancient games, such as Chess and Go, and more modern counterparts, such as Labyrinth and Set.

"Judson *lost*." Oran flapped his hand. "That's why we're on our way to B5 for cleanup. So, yes, I'm fairly confident he made a mistake at the hour and thirteen minute mark."

Imani shook her head. She'd watched Judson's career flourish from a teen competing in junior tournaments to a full-time Player representing the Antarctican Republic on the international stage, both in friendly and hostile games. Like the one he'd just died for. A territorial spat over a popular oceanic trade route that would generate significant income via shipping taxes to whoever controlled it. A conflict that, in the past, would've incited a years-long war, costing billions in the economy, destroyed valuable infrastructure, and scarred the environment for decades. Instead, it was all civilly resolved within three hours, at the mere cost of Judson and the unlucky citizens in B5. (An unfortunate necessity; but actions must yield consequences or else they wouldn't mean much.)

"Judson's mistake was at the hour and thirty-seven mark." Imani switched the channel to the private livestream of Custodian drones zipping through the streets of B5. She'd released the drones the moment B5's fate was determined. "Dirkin's Corner was a feint to establish control over the midline, which Niko was too experienced to fall for but didn't endanger Judson's position either. Judson retreating to the quarter board instead of trying to surround his opponent's frontline at the hour thirty-seven was what allowed Niko to seize control and win."

Oran stared at Imani for a long second. "Damn, why weren't you picked to train as a Player? You're a strategic genius—"

"I was never screened." At Oran's confused expression, Imani sighed. He'd joined the Custodians a couple months ago and was clearly oblivious to her ... unusual upbringing. "I spent the first thirteen years of my life in the Grand Arrival Compound before the government dismantled it. They didn't bother screening any of the minors for Player potential before sending them to the state schools."

"Shit, wasn't Grand Arrival that—"

"—cult waiting for aliens to beam them up to a mothership for a journey to their next home world because this one was corrupted beyond repair? Yeah, that's the one."

"I thought that cult fell apart when its leader died."

"It didn't fall apart." Imani curled her upper lip. "It *destroyed* itself when rival factions started setting off bombs and engaging in a shootout so egregious the government finally intervened—and good riddance."

She shuddered, imagining her life if she were still trapped within that 100-acre compound in the middle of the desert. Petty fights for food and medicine. Communication blackouts from the outside world. Blatant rejection of the Battle Games because they turned life into a "game," thereby making a mockery out of the universe's most divine gift.

That had been the biggest lie, Imani discovered shortly after reintegrating with society. The Battle

Games *preserved* life. By mediating conflicts and maintaining peace, the Games allowed life to flourish and reach its full potential.

"Karlo's looking hungry," Kit murmured, and all attention swung back to the small screen, split into eight squares for the eight drones tracking the pink fog.

"The winds are helping it spread," Imani noted. She could practically smell the burnt sugar scent that accompanied the mist, lingering in the cracks and crevices of infrastructure long after Karlo dissipated.

The crew fell silent, watching the ocean of death Karlo left in its wake. Supposedly, it was a painless way to die—neurotoxins shut down the nervous system and flooded the brain with an overdose of melanide.

Just like falling asleep to the sweetest dreams, Peaceful Ends had promised when it pitched Karlo to the fledgling International Conflict Resolution Court. *Dignity in death.*

Imani wasn't sure if *dignity* was the right term for the bodies collapsed on the streets, like drunkards passed out after an overtaxing night. But at least they weren't riddled with bullet holes like the bodies in the compound shootout's aftermath.

A pack of pigeons swirled into flight, startled by Karlo's approach. Two cats wobbled down a brick wall, dazed but otherwise unharmed from inhaling the fog; they would recover within the hour. From a stalled car, a dog pawed at its owner then whined when they didn't wake up. The stop light blinked green.

The world moved on.

CHAPTER 3
NIKO

WHEN HE WAS YOUNGER, NIKO DIDN'T understand what a "bittersweet victory" meant. As far as his eight-year-old self was concerned, victory was sweet like strawberries and summer ripe peaches and rich hot chocolate during the chilled months. When he won his first junior championship at the International Peacetime Games, he celebrated with a decadent apple cake.

Then he turned eighteen and started participating in Battle Games, and began to taste the *bitterness*. Sure, he still felt the heady rush of relief and thrill that came from winning, but it was heavy with understanding that it came at a price.

Lately, Niko's victories skewed more bitter than sweet, even as his fame grew and his name became a household staple. He was, as far as the Archipelago citizens were concerned, a walking legend, a defender, a symbol of national pride.

And his latest Battle Game win had only solidified

his status as an icon.

The night breeze nipped at Niko's exposed skin. Cameras flashed in his face until silver orbs floated across his vision. He waved at the reporters crowded outside of the post-Game party then rushed into the lounge, escaping the ceaseless questions he'd been answering mindlessly, spewing carefully scripted answers.

"Daton, from the Global Reporter." A middle-aged man with slicked back hair flashed a press badge then shoved a cam-mic into Niko's face. "So, how does it feel to tie the world record for the highest number of Battle Games won?"

Niko pasted on a smile and supplied the expected response. "Happy, of course. But more importantly, grateful and appreciative of everyone who enabled this victory for the Atlantic Archipelago Nation—my teammates, managers, coaches, and more."

"Ah, speaking of Coach Ivonna ... how is she feeling about you *this* close to breaking her record?" He winked and leaned in. "Don't be afraid us how she *really* feels, I just know everyone's hungry for some family rivalry."

Disdain dripped through Niko as he resisted the urge to sneer at Daton's blatant fishing for gossip-column content. Gods, he wanted to scream at the sky. *Is no one else bothered that thousands of people died because their square was selected by a code?* Instead, he maintained composure. Pretend everything was okay even as anxiety sharpened its claws on his nerves, scraping his temper ragged. "I'm sure Coach Ivonna is happy for my recent accomplishment. There is no family rivalry between us—she's always my coach first and foremost, mother in whatever time and space is left."

The utility-band on his left wrist buzzed as the timer went off, and he bit back a relieved groan. He pointedly raised his hand in an apologetic wave, flashing the still-vibrating utility-band. "Sorry, but I've got to go."

With that, he finally fled the flashing lights and forest of cam-mics and rushed into the reserved lounge.

It wasn't much better inside. Music blasted so loud not even his noise-canceling earbuds could mitigate the thumping bass, and at least two hundred guests swarmed the bar and dance floor. Ivonna cut through the crowd like a sharking slicing through water, gracefully falling in step beside Niko and passed him a glass of sparkling lemon water. She didn't permit alcohol. Why give yourself a disadvantage by killing off brain cells for your opponents?

"That was quick," she commented.

"It was twenty minutes."

"Did you talk to—"

"Yes. I spent at least two minutes with company representatives from Peaceful Ends, SafeShields, and Pureyre. In return for promotional pictures with their reps, SafeShields will be installing upgraded bunkers at the family farm this week, and Pureyre is donating a month's worth of Grade 1000 air filters."

Ivonna nodded, then slid Niko a tiny smile that caught him off guard. "You've done good."

Translation: *I'm proud of you.*

"As a Player," she said, "you're expected to put your life on the line for the wellbeing of the nation. But even more important, you're also in the best position to protect the family." A thoughtful crease folded across her brow. "You know, that was my primary motivation as a Player back then—not pride or representing the country or even my own survival—but protecting the family, *our* family.."

Niko nodded even as something vaguely resembling shame and guilt soured the roof of his mouth. He knew family was something to be cherished, protected, loved . . . and yet, he couldn't muster the same depth of caring toward them that Ivonna harbored. Maybe it's because as a coach, she had more freedom and could visit the family farm a couple times each month, or maybe it's because she'd grown up with memories running through the orchards with her siblings, whereas Niko's childhood memories comprised of the academy grounds and late nights studying taped Games.

When Niko thought of family, he thought of Aiden Tays. In fact, the only thing that kept Niko at the party instead of retreating to his apartment was the promise of seeing him later tonight. The only person who truly saw Niko for who he was, who he *wanted* to be, instead of the sanitized version known by the public.

"Ten Battle Game victories!" Ganjee exclaimed, snapping Niko out of his wandering thoughts. The junior teammate threw a handful of biodegradable glitter, eliciting cheers from those nearby. "I want to reach double digits, too."

Niko chuckled tightly. "Well, if the Archipelago keeps waging war, you'll get your chance. At the rate our leaders are getting involved in international disputes, there'll be plenty of Games for you to play in."

The laughter around him dialed down a notch. Niko hid a grim smile behind a sip of his drink, edible glitter sticking to the back of his throat.

Thanks to power Players such as Ivonna in the last decade, and now Niko at the helm, the Archipelago had increased its territory size by 15%, doubled its net wealth, and spread the national religion of Second Wave Hinduism to every major country, all in an astonishingly short period of time. Most talks at the international table resolved with the Archipelago holding the better deal since so few countries wanted to risk a worse outcome in a Battle Game. And those who *did* push things to the game board, well, Niko always ensured the Archipelago came out on top.

The swell of resentment that breached through his meandering thoughts caught Niko off guard. He was a *Player*, goddamit, so why did he feel like he was nothing more than a pawn? Nothing more than a marionette on invisible strings—

"Go," Coach Ivonna ordered quietly.

A few teammates slunk off to find more upbeat company, and when Ivonna flicked a hand, the remaining ones scattered.

Niko clenched his jaw. "Thanks, but you didn't have—"

She waved away his words. "Don't worry about it, we're family and look out for each other."

That would've been a nice and warm sentiment if she'd ended right there, but Coach Ivonna was many things and *warm and nice* were not any of them. *Warm and nice* would've seen her end up as yet another dead Player.

She continued, "It's a bad look if you're dismissive of your own teammates. We need to maintain your image to keep sponsorships strong."

That earlier surge of resentment flared like a grenade

inside Niko, a supernova of thorns and shards exploding inside his chest. He forced himself to relax and scrub all traces of irritation out of his tone. "You're my coach, and I'll listen to you when it comes to gameplay and dealing with public appearances. But stay out of my personal life. I can handle my own teammates."

"I was only looking out for you, as family."

Family. That bleeding word again. "Thanks, Coach, but I can take care of myself."

Hurt flickered across Ivonna's face.

Niko sighed. She'd meant well, and he didn't intend to upset her. But he also couldn't stop that tight, prickly feeling from expanding under his ribs. It took all his strength to smile and capitulate, "You're right. I'm irritated, tired, and socially drained. I think, for everyone's sake, I'll head home for the night."

He turned and caught a familiar flash in his periphery. There. That familiar, bleached-blond hair and purposeful stride, as if the man entering through the room was ready to take on the world. And in a way, he was, one revolution at a time.

"Niko snapped his gaze away before she could follow his line of sight. "Manager Barlow wants to discuss strategies for the next batch of trainees. Can you let him know I'm not feeling well and will find him tomorrow?"

She gave him a long look, and he was half convinced she saw through his ploy to divert her, but ultimately nodded and vanished outside. The tightness in Niko's chest unraveled a few turns now that he wasn't under her imposing watch. He pushed a hand through his hair then hurried toward—

"Aiden," he greeted, slipping beside his—Boyfriend? Partner? Lover?—Niko didn't know what to label them.

Aiden's head swiveled, taking in the dripping sea glass chandelier, the strobing lavender lights, and delicacies almost too pretty to eat circulating on waiter bot trays. "Well, this is fancier than Bar None."

Niko crooked a smile at the mention of their preferred haunt. "I prefer Bar None. Less noisy and heartier food." He paused, soaking in Aiden's presence. It'd been weeks since they last met, since Aiden's job often had him inaccessible for stretches of time. Hopefully, he would soon be joining Aiden on those jobs. "There's a balcony where we can talk. I've already scoped it for mics and cams, and it's clean."

The two of them efficiently circumvented the masses without attracting too much attention by sticking to the perimeter. Niko only had to stop twice to accept congratulations from partygoers before he was stepping out onto the balcony overlooking the courtyard. The sliding door hissed shut, darkened glass shielding them from view.

"I've missed you," Niko confessed. It felt weird, admitting his feelings out loud. But for Aiden, he would. He wanted to.

The corners of Aiden's green eyes softened. "I've missed you, too, and have been worried sick about your last Game. Though I see now I had nothing to worry about. Congrats with the win."

Niko's mouth twisted. "Stop. Don't congratulate me for participating in such a disgusting practice."

Fuck. It felt *good* to say that out loud.

"Congratulations on surviving another day." Aiden

took a step closer, and Niko inhaled a shaky breath that turned into a sigh when Aiden touched his jaw with precious tenderness. "Is that better?"

"Much." Niko turned to press a kiss against Aiden's palm.

Aiden pulled Niko into a hug, squeezing so tight all the air rushed out of Niko's lungs. Or maybe it was Aiden's proximity that did that. Aiden's mere presence tended to have that effect.

"So, this is where you live, huh?" Aiden loosened his embrace but didn't fully let go, dancing his fingers up and down Niko's back.

Sparks shot down his shoulder blades as he toyed with Aiden's curls, resisting the urge to close his eyes as he intoned, "Welcome to the Battle Team Campus. My home for . . . pretty much my entire life."

"It's beautiful. I miss the traditional Archipelago architecture when I travel."

Niko gazed out toward the campus expanse. The buildings and walkways spiraled in hypnotizing patterns, illuminated by solar powered light orbs and slow churning breeze spinners. Native plants adorned the courtyard and colorful vines hugged the south-facing side of many buildings in a living wallpaper, carefully curated into swirls. "All the Fibonacci inspired designs make me dizzy if I stare at them for too long. Where have you been traveling to?"

Aiden's hand paused at Niko's lower back, then started to tap out a sequence. Tap. Tap. Tap tap. Tap tap tap. Tap tap tap tap tap.

"Smartass," Niko grumbled fondly.

"I've been here and there."

"How descriptive."

"Work stuff. Confidential stuff."

"Is it your work *work* or your other work?"

"Both, Niko."

He knew that, of course. Aiden was a government employee by day, in a position that required discreetness, and by night he operated with the Iconoclasts to overthrow the very government he worked for.

Much as he loathed to, Niko forced himself to disentangle from Aiden. "Take me on your next trip."

"I don't think you'd find my job very interesting."

"Not your day job. The other one." Niko braced his shoulders and firmed his voice. "I'm ready to join the Iconoclasts. Been ready for a while."

"You might be ready, but the others aren't."

He groaned. "What's the big deal with bringing me on board? If you were able to join as a government official, why can't I?"

Aiden reached for Niko, but he stepped back, refusing to be pulled under Aiden's mesmerizing spell. Sighing, Aiden rocked back on his heels, eyes flashing with equal parts exasperation and endearment. This was an argument they'd hashed out more than once, and Aiden had unfailingly delivered the same response each time. "I was born into the Iconoclasts, Niko. My job with the government was handpicked by the organization so they could have an insider."

"I bet there are other government officials part of the Iconoclasts whose parents weren't founding members."

"True, but there's also a huge difference between inducting your run-of-the-mill government employee and an internationally famous Player. Fact is, a lot of members see you as a risk."

Niko tensed his jaw. He knew Aiden was the only reason the Iconoclasts were even *considering* letting him join. "Why bother telling me about the Iconoclasts, if you're so determined to keep me away from them?"

"Because when I saw you at Bar None two years ago, I saw the first inklings of dissatisfaction with the Games from a Player who should've loved everything about them."

Obviously, Niko hadn't known about Aiden's extracurricular involvements when they'd first met. It had taken half a year before Aiden even mentioned the existence of the radical group seeking to overthrow the Battle Games, and that was only after many meetups where Aiden painstakingly teased out Niko's most treacherous thoughts.

"What do I have to do to convince the others to let me join?" Niko allowed a pleading thread to stitch through his voice. A lump rose in the back of his throat as he gripped the balcony handrail, knuckles painted soft red from the bulbs strung from the awning. "Tens of thousands of lives decimated today by this stupid, *stupid* Game."

"It's not your fault."

"I could have lost."

"And citizens would've still been murdered—just Archipelago lives instead of Antarcticans. It's a lose-lose situation."

"Truth," Niko agreed darkly. He slid Aiden a sideways glance, the corners of his lips ticking up. "You know, my name wasn't supposed to be Niko. That was a typo. I was supposed to be Nike, after the goddess of victory. Except Ivonna has terrible handwriting, and the hospital thought the *e* was an *o,* and put Niko into the registration."

"She didn't want to make a correction?"

"Guess not. And she was extra glad of her choice when I tested into the Battle Team program—said Nike would've been too on the nose."

Aiden hummed in the back of his throat. "I prefer Niko."

"Me too. It stands for *victory of the people.*" He locked eyes with Aiden, brown clashing against green. "Not victory for a political entity, but for the *people,* like what the Iconoclasts are fighting for."

A fiery determination burned low in Niko's gut. A call to arms, a visceral desire to join the elusive rebels that had been causing ripples underground. He wanted to be part of the rebellion so badly it was a nauseous ache. Although he wasn't so vain to believe him single-handedly joining the Iconoclasts would induce any note-worthy effects, he was confident he could contribute somehow, some way. Even the smallest splash could incite the biggest ripples.

"I wish they would retire me," Niko muttered.

"Well, they *did* retire Ivonna after her tenth Game," Aiden mused. "Have you heard from the higher ups?"

"No."

"Maybe she's convinced the Managers to keep you playing for as long as possible. I wouldn't put it past her, considering how much her family benefits from your status."

Niko shook his head, though that didn't stop the

drop of inky doubt from spreading. "She wouldn't do that." At least he hoped so.

Aiden scowled. "Ivonna has no qualms overstepping boundaries. Being your mother doesn't grant her the right to control your life."

"Regardless, the Managers only retired her due to public pressure. There would've been vicious backlash if they hadn't given her the opportunity to step down after being the first Player to survive ten Battle Games, and even more so when she dropped that pregnancy bombshell on live news." She'd been twenty-seven, and four months pregnant with Niko. He gestured at himself and scoffed. "There are no perks to being the second person to achieve something. Coming in second is just being the first loser."

"Hey, drop the attitude."

He rolled his eyes.

Aiden patted his arm. "A couple more years, then you can retire."

Thirty-years-old was the internationally agreed-upon age when Players must retire. Some archaic attempt of keeping the field as even as possible in terms of experience.

"I don't know if I can last a couple more years." Niko's whispered words were meant for himself but Aiden overheard all the same, and frowned.

"If you think the Battle Games are an ugly affair, then you haven't seen what a revolution entails."

"I don't care. I'm tired of living this farce. I want to *live* for something I believe in. I want to be part of something bigger, better, *brighter*." Niko raised his chin, confidence strumming in his every fiber only to collapse half a beat later. His words were jagged glass shards crunching in his molars. "I can't keep on playing. The weight of it all is—" He pressed a hand against his sternum, chest tightening in a vice. "Sometimes, I hear them. The voices of those lost to the fog. When I'm jogging on the trails or practicing in the training facilities or lying in my room at night."

Aiden pushed out a rough breath and straightened his posture, capturing Niko's hand between his. "Once you join the Iconoclasts, there is no going back. The moment you learn the faces of other members, names, sensitive information, you're locked in for life."

Hope sparked through Niko as he turned to face Aiden. "I understand."

"*Do* you?" Aiden tilted his head, a curl of hair flopping across his forehead. "A revolution can be a bloody, dirty monster. A beast that demands sacrifices. Don't romanticize a revolution, Niko. That's a surefire path to losing your way."

Niko leaned in and brushed his lips against Aiden's. Citrus and cinnamon lingered on his tongue, the flavors of those little honey-colored candies Aiden loved. "You're my compass," he whispered against Aiden's lips. "I won't get lost with you by my side."

Aiden kissed him back with force, hands slipping behind to cradle Niko's face. Molten heat seeped between them, setting Niko's body ablaze. He nosed his way down Aiden's neck, imparting sharp, nipping kisses. He savored Aiden's response, the way his breaths shallowed and heart pounded against his own chest.

"We could have this every day," Niko murmured, "if I joined the Iconoclasts." Despite his celebrity status, nearly every aspect of his life was carefully monitored, restricted. The nation couldn't have their top Player getting incapacitated, whether by accident or malicious intent. He gripped Aiden's shoulders, nails digging with emphasis. "Being a Player is going to kill me. Get me out of here. Free me, please."

"Okay."

Niko froze.

"I will," Aiden promised.

"For real?"

"For real." Aiden angled his head, lips grazing Niko's temple in a fleeting kiss. "You'll have to pass an initiation test to prove your trustworthiness. The organization needs to know you'll follow orders, no questions asked."

"Tell me what to do."

His breath was hot against Niko's ear. "I need you to play one last Game."

AFTER TWELVE HOURS HAD PASSED FROM Karlo's release into B5, Imani and her crew were given the go-ahead to initiate clean up. They donned their haz suits and respirators, flung open the van doors, and began methodically clearing the square. Bodies were identified, tagged, and bagged. Once the casualty list was officially released, family members could request either a state-standard eco-cremation service, or for their loved ones to be sent to a private funeral.

"Population of 62,823," Imani murmured into her comms as she peeled back the eyelid of an elderly woman to scan her retina. Her handheld identifier added Mariah Johassa under the deceased list. "Hopefully other Custodian crews already have boots on the ground."

"This is an affluent square," Oran mused. "Which means there'll be more bunkers per capita. Assuming the bunkers are filled to max capacity, we're probably looking at roughly 30,000 victims."

"They're all victims, even those who got into a

bunker," Kit replied. Their location tracker placed their pip a couple blocks down the street. "They've still lost friends and family."

"But they're *alive*." Imani wrenched open a car door with a job-issued universal lock override (*Ulo,* she'd fondly named the nifty gadget). It was one of her most valuable possessions. Each lock swipe was logged and monitored, to prevent Ulo from being used for less scrupulous purposes. Her supervisor had made very clear what would happen if Ulo was used illegally: an internal alarm would notify nearby authorities of the breach location, she would be charged for trespassing, and lose her job.

"Yeah, but *everyone* could be alive, not just those who made it into a bunker," Kit countered.

"As in . . . not release Karlo?" Oran asked. He was a couple blocks down the street, prying open the doors of a hydro-cell bus. "And only have the Player die?"

"Exactly!" Kit exclaimed. "We can keep the Battle Games as a form of conflict resolution, but minus the whole *killing millions of people* part."

"Get rid of Karlo, and we'll be out of a job." Imani scanned the ID chips implanted behind the ears of the vehicle's two occupants. *Minnie Kingson, age 43, AI coder. Leona Kingson, age 44, veterinarian.* "Anyway, no one would take the Games seriously if it didn't carry consequences. And judging by history, the Battle Games have maintained international stability pretty damn well when you consider the alternative." She gestured at the self-sustaining buildings and magnificent solar spires stretching toward the sky. "This whole city would've been bombed to bits, the water contaminated with toxins, and the land uninhabitable for years, if not decades. A complete waste of resources and infrastructure."

Within the week, Redistributors would come through and re-allocate the various properties (vehicles, real estate, tech, et cetera) to best-fit matches on waitlists. It only made sense to do so. A major reason why Earth was almost irrevocably destroyed by earlier generations was the insatiable stripping of the planet's resources. Since Battle Games allowed infrastructure to be reused, it'd also alleviated the housing crisis, eradicated famine, and cleared overflowing landfills among other problems of the past.

"Hm." A challenging lilt entered Kit's voice. "You think carrying out systematic murders is somehow better than the chaos of traditional warfare?"

Imani sighed and humored their penchant for debate. "It's systematically *random*. Nobody can predict which square will be fogged. The enemy is no longer purposely targeting capital cities or contested territory. The whole beauty of Karlo is that it's an equal opportunity event."

"Not true." Kit grunted, and the muffled *thump* of something heavy thudding onto the floor sounded from their background. (Probably a body.) "The wealthy have private bunkers and escape drones to evac—"

"There'll always be people exempt from the rules. At least the Battle Games mitigates those exemptions," Oran interjected. "You're beating a dead goat."

"It's horse," Kit said.

"What?"

"Thank you, Oran, for speaking some sense." Imani maneuvered the AI coder and veterinarian into a bamboo fiber body bag with practiced ease. Then she scanned the barcode printed at the foot, uploading its location for pick up later. "Kit, you're starting to tread on treacherous grounds."

"Aw, come on," they whined. "I'm just keeping the conversation interesting."

"If you keep up that shit-stirring, you're going to end up with a mouthful."

But then again, she had yet to see Kit eat shit, so maybe they were cannier than she credited them to be. At any rate, the crew was used to Kit playing devil's advocate, and knew their incorrigible teammate enjoyed their daily exercise in the form of walking the line between treason and controversy.

Motion flickered in Imani's periphery. She whirled toward the movement but spotted nothing. Weird. She slammed the car door shut then worked her way to the next vehicle on the solar roadway. A finely-tuned EMP blast had been released along with Karlo, which turned off the engines in all of the cars and anything else electrically powered that didn't have an auto-reboot.

The door was locked on this van, its windows tinted so dark she couldn't make out its occupants. Imani unclipped Ulo from her belt and pressed the gadget against the front door. Ulo's indicator light blinked green as the swipe was logged into its records, then a chime sounded when the van's lock disengaged. Imani's haz lights automatically turned on when she stuck her head inside the dark cabin.

A whole family had fallen asleep, then into death. A Custodian with less experience might've felt sadness or guilt.

Imani only felt relief and gratitude.

Societal stability came at a cost, and this was a price she was more than willing to pay. Even before the Grand Arrival fractured into two factions—one wanting to continue waiting for the mothership, the other desiring to take matters into their own hands via the bright idea of storming a government facility to steal a rocket or something—life at the compound had been full of uncertainties and infighting. Power lines often went down, harvests would be bad, and medicine shortages were more common than not.

Sacrificing random squares to Karlo so everyone else could have unlimited clean water, accessible healthcare, and reliable shelter? A more than fair deal.

"Look, maybe the Battle Games aren't perfect," Imani conceded. "But it's the best solution we have."

"Solution to *what?*" Kit was all too eager to resume their debate.

"Resource management. Population control. Conflict resolution. The world's biggest problems." She tagged and bagged the family. When she looked back down the road, dozens of biodegradable body bags lined the sidewalk like shrines to ancient deities. Sacrifices to Karlo. "The Battle Games aren't a magical panacea with no side effects, but it's the best we have and that's good enough."

"Good enough, huh?" Imani wasn't sure if she imagined the grim undercurrent in Kit's response, but then their chuckle burst into her earpiece. "Is that what you say when trying a new recipe and it tastes mediocre but it's *good enough* so you continue making it?"

"Whoa now, you're comparing apples to peaches."

"Oranges, Imani."

She bit back a smile. "First off, modifying a recipe is *far* easier than modifying international peace accords. Second, how dare you imply I would ever cook something that tastes subpar?"

Cooking was the first true joy Imani had discovered and carried throughout her life. Back in the compound, lack of spices and scarce ingredients had forced her to be creative in coming up with new and interesting meals. Now, her neighborhood grocery store carried a dependably varied stock of local and exotic foods for her to experiment with.

"I didn't say it tasted bad," Kit protested. "Just . . . mediocre. Like the protein bars that come in ration kits."

"If it's mediocre, then it's *not* good enough." She hopped onto the sidewalk, taking reprieve in the shade provided by the glossy-leafed birch trees. The midday sun had begun its blaze in earnest, and sweat stung her eyes, salted the corners of her lips when she licked them. "Life is too short to eat mediocre food."

"Agreed." Kit appeared around the corner and waved. "That's why we don't settle for mediocrity. Complacency is the death of progress."

Imani narrowed her eyes and marched toward them. "Stop trying to make a point, Kit."

"What do you mean?" they asked innocently.

"*Kit.*"

They threw both hands into the air in mock surrender, then pointed to the looming building off the side. "Want to tackle the hospital together?"

She nodded, then frowned as they approached the main entrance. The revolving door spun in silent invitation. "The power should've been shut down."

Kit dismissed her unease with a shrug and strode through the entryway. "Maybe there's an internal power bank."

She followed them in. The back of her neck prickled, and when she glanced behind, the door slowly came to a stop. She blinked, then chalked it up to the wind—a final parting breath from Karlo.

"Somebody's been here recently." imani's heart pulsed in the back of her throat, spooked by the overhead lights illuminating the empty hospital corridor. Motion-activated lights that had already turned on before she and Kit had even set foot in the hall. "We should send an alert to the local enforcement hub."

"I bet another Custodian team already swept through this building." Kit poked their head into an exam room, gestured it was empty, then moved to open the next door with their universal lock override. A beat passed as they scoped out the room. "Ah, we got half a dozen here."

"No other team's in the vicinity." Imani stuck her utility-band with the city map displayed out toward them. Yellow pips marked the locations of other Custodians. Kit and Imani were the only ones in this block.

"Well, unless there's a zombie wandering the streets of Nova City, it's probably just a power glitch. Some surge from the generator that temporarily reset the hospital's system." Kit braced the door open and unclipped the handheld scanner from their belt. "Karlo would've killed off anyone not in a bunker or safe house."

Imani shook her head and followed Kit into the recovery ward. The patients in here wouldn't be recovering ever. A prickle spread between her shoulder blades as she stepped up to the first cot. Hospitals were where lives were saved, but this one had turned into a mausoleum. A decade working as a Custodian and she still found clearing hospitals the most unnerving part of her job.

She lifted the eyelid of the patient—body—and scanned the man's retina. Her gaze flickered to the medical instruments positioned beside the cot. The monitors and air canisters (a proprietary blend infused with medicine to facilitate healing) were all marked with the Peaceful Ends logo. Although the company was best known for being the manufacturer of Karlo, Peaceful Ends also consumed a large slice of the medical industry pie and had partnerships with most major hospitals.

The scanner beeped. *Vila Skyore, age 28, teacher.* Imani logged the ID under the deceased list. She glanced back at the silent monitors clustered around each cot like mourners at a grave. "It's not a power surge, or else all the devices plugged into the outlets would've restarted. Something's wrong . . . tampered with."

Tap tap tap.

She froze. The sound—footsteps—came from the hall outside. Her nape prickled with alarm, and she bolted toward the door.

"Imani, wait!"

Kit's frantic shout punctured her comms piece as she swung her gaze down the length of the corridor. The lights flickered on past the window panes on the next set of double doors. Sweat beaded along her hairline as her instincts battled against her mind. Her muscles twitched to escape. The walls were leering in onto her, the roof on the verge of collapsing—and even as her brain reasoned this was all in her imagination, she couldn't help but shudder at the echoes of gunfire popping against her eardrums. She needed to run, to hide, to—

"Imani!" Kit waved a hand in front of her visor.

She snapped out of the flashback with a jolt. This wasn't the Grand Arrival compound. This was Nova City Hospital, and there was an intruder on the loose.

"Call for backup!" Imani barked and beelined toward the double doors on trembling legs. With each step, she shoved back memories of the compound and grounded herself in the present—on her heart bucking inside her ribcage, rubber soles squeaking against the tiles, and sweat salting her lips.

By the time she rounded the corner, her legs were steady and she managed to glimpse a figure ducking into the stairwell. The person was dressed in all black and wore a respirator that definitely wasn't one of the rated models. Idiot was going to get themselves killed. "Hey, you! This is an active contaminant zone! You can't be here!"

Of course that only made them sprint even faster. She growled under her breath and bolted down the stairs, cursing as the distance between them increased with each level they descended. How deep *did* this hospital go? At least it was easy to know where the intruder was headed, thanks to the ominous click of each set of motion-triggered lights switching on.

"Hey," Kit panted, catching up to her with their leggy strides, "boss says to fall back!"

"Why are they headed for the basement storage facilities?" Imani muttered, still focused on the intruder

Her lungs heaved and sweat pooled at her nape. Running in a haz suit was worse than cooking with expired ingredients.

"We shouldn't be here." Kit grabbed Imani's arm and grounded to a halt. She shot them a glower. They were wasting precious time and the culprit was going to get away. "Safety protocol dictates law enforcement—"

BOOM!

A sudden flash ripped through the air. The air punched out of Imani's lungs. She dropped to a crouch, panic flaring through her nerves, tucking her chin against her chest with hands clasped behind her neck. She squeezed her eyes shut to ward against the silver starbursts blinding her vision. Her teeth chattered and her shoulders shook, shivers wrenching through her body in spastic jerks.

No, no, no.

She was back in the closet, in the dark, violence unfurling its savage cruelty to the symphony of screams and explosions. Humanity left to its ingrained brutality.

"Come on, Imani." She felt Kit tug on her arm once more, firm but not unkindly.

She squinted, struggling to ground herself amidst the smoke curling out the far end of the T-junction, thickest by a door marked with the Peaceful Ends logo.

"Let's get out of here," Kit said, helping her to her feet.

This time, she didn't resist as they led her out of the hospital.

BREAKING NEWS: EXPLOSION
ROCKS NOVA CITY HOSPITAL
IN FOGGING AFTERMATH

GLOBAL REPORTER: NO CASUALTIES
REPORTED IN NOVA CITY HOSPITAL
BOMBING ASIDE FROM BLOWN
OFF VAULT DOOR

GLOBAL REPORTER: INVESTIGATIONS
INDICATE THE ICONOCLAST REBEL
GROUP RESPONSIBLE FOR NOVA CITY
HOSPITAL VAULT BREAK-IN—BUT
WHAT ARE THEY LOOKING FOR?

CHAPTER 5
NIKO

BY AGE SEVEN, NIKO HAD MASTERED *THE mask.* It was his Game face, one that made world-class poker players jealous and could trick a facial lie detector AI.

By age seventeen, Niko regularly ranked top three in the International Junior Battle Games League.

By age twenty-seven, Niko had taken home eight Peacetime Games Championship trophies and resolved ten conflicts between the Atlantic Archipelago Nation and other countries. He'd won all of his Battle Games, of course, considering he was still alive and currently in the final quarter of Atlantic Archipelago Nation vs Central American Alliance: disagreement over greenhouse pollution allowances.

By age twenty-seven and a half, Niko was experiencing his first chance of a certain death. All for a chance to join the Iconoclasts.

The game of choice was Humanity's Race, and he was losing by a point. Three minutes left on the clock.

I don't want to die.

Words he'd spoken earlier this week, when he found out he'd been called to the board again. Words that now marched through his thoughts like a pair of muddy combat boots.

I won't let you die, Aiden had soothed, the two of them tucked away in a corner table at Bar None.

Niko slid his Scientist game piece over two squares. Winced when the opponent countered it *and* placed her own Scientist in a position poised to wipe out half of his Food Producers and Politicians.

Live to play, play to win, and yet we all win to die at the end of the day, Niko had groused.

When Aiden had shared the Iconoclasts' ideology with Niko, he'd been immediately obsessed. The ideas captivated Niko's mind like lightning seizing the skies, electrified his senses, jolted him to the possibility of a different future. A future that now amped up a current of hope charging through his veins. A future where those who incited conflict *also* reaped the consequences. That was only fair, and wasn't the whole point of the Battle Games to be *fair?*

What if you didn't win to die, but died to win? Aiden proposed.

Adrenaline shivered down Niko's spine. *Is this a hint about my initiation test?*

I'm not allowed to say. Yet Aiden winked all the same.

I—I'm not ready to die.

Aiden's gaze softened. *And you won't.*

Another stab of panic speared through Niko. He wasn't used to second guessing himself, but standing on the banks of no return, doubt wrapped its bony fingers around his ankles, threatening to drag him into the waters. *What I'm supposed to do during my next Game—it won't . . . will there . . .*

Casualties will be minimized, Aiden promised. *Just do your job, and I'll see you on the other side.*

An image of a dark, wide river flowed into Niko's mind. He exhaled, slow and controlled. He was prepared to leave his—Ivonna's—family in pursuit of a better future. The family would be well off for decades, Niko had seen to that, and Ivonna could finally retire from Coaching to spend more time with them. Him leaving was for the best. *Okay.*

By age twenty-seven and a half, Niko threw his first Game, and his opponent swept the final purple game piece off the board.

So this is how it feels to lose. Niko's face betrayed none of the emotional turmoil flipping through his stomach as the stadium lights flashed red and yellow, the national colors of the Central American Alliance. *But sometimes you've got to lose something to gain something.*

That was the balance of nature.

Recycled confetti in poppy red and sunshine yellow fluttered down while the crowd exploded into celebratory roars and solemn silence. The gamecasters screamed something unintelligible, static noise merging into a deafening din. Referee guards marched out, but instead of circling his opponent as Niko was accustomed to, they surrounded him this time.

The next few minutes passed in a hallucinatory dream. Snapshot moments forever etched into his neural pathways.

The victor pumping her arm with a ferocious grin plastered on her face.

Click.

Fifty-thousand bitter eyes staring down at Niko from the purple section of the stands.

Click.

A map of the Archipelago lit up on the screen, the islands divided into seven-hundred and twenty-nine squares. A map he never wanted to see on the big-screen pixels.

Click.

The Referees closing in on him, shock rifles primed, as the purple square flitted across the gridded map. The helmets masked the Referees' faces, hiding away their expressions and identities. Human robots impartial to Niko's plight.

I don't want to die. Niko had never been so sure of a sentiment in his twenty-seven-and-a-half years. The desperation to live burned bright through his veins, solar flares blazing through his body.

I won't let you die. He clung onto Aiden's promise like a dying man clinging onto life.

Click.

The crowd chanting the countdown. *I know someone who can hack the system.* Aiden's mossy voice was a calming reminder as anxiety poked pin-holes into Niko's skin.

Click.

The purple square landed on F37. Niko hid a sharp breath, too well-trained to betray his true emotions, even with fear raking its claws down his insides.

F37, his home city, where his family lived. A small

city within a sparsely populated grid.

Casualties will be minimized.

The promise had been kept, just not in the way Niko expected. Sweat creased in his palms as he swayed to his feet, focusing on the facts to maintain composure. His family had the newest bunker system, thanks to his sponsorship with SafeShields. The family would be safe. Karlo wouldn't hurt them. *Couldn't* hurt them.

Click.

A Referee wearing the captain's armband approached. Niko steadied his stance. If he was going to die, he wanted to die on his feet. Niko's gaze widened as the captain removed the tint on the helmet, revealing a strip of his face through the clear bioplastic

Click.

The trigger was pulled. Voltage arced through his heart. Familiar green eyes stared back at him as Niko collapsed into darkness, the sound of waves lapping at his ears.

GLOBAL REPORTER: FORMER
PEACETIME GAMES CHAMPION
NIKO VANDES FINALLY BESTED
BY GALLIA SUMMS

LIVE FROM THE STADIUM: NIKO
VANDES (OR AT LEAST HIS BODY)
IS MISSING—COULD HE BE ALIVE?

UPDATE ON THE NIKO VANDES
CASE: OFFICIALS ANNOUNCE VANDES'
CITIZEN ID CHIP DESTROYED

UPDATE ON THE NIKO VANDES
CASE: NIKO VANDES DECLARED
A MISSING PERSON AND WANTED
FUGITIVE BY THE INTERNATIONAL
CONFLICT RESOLUTION COURT—
STORY CURRENTLY DEVELOPING.

GLOBAL REPORTER: FORMER
REFEREE GUARD CAPTAIN AIDEN
TAYS WANTED FOR CONSPIRACY
AGAINST INTERNATIONAL PEACE

CHAPTER 6

NIKO

THE SCENT OF PINE HIT NIKO'S SENSES. His entire body ached, muscles sore like he'd run up a mountain with a fifty kilogram pack. A coppery tang lingered in his mouth. His brain blanked, struggling to comprehend what was happening. He breathed in deep, saturating his lungs with crisp, cool air, though the movement caused a spasm through his chest.

"*—preliminary reports state a tragic glitch at the Vandes family farm is responsible for—*"

Niko flicked open his eyes. Weathered wooden rafters crossed overhead. A window allowed glimpses to the mountainous landscape outside. In his periphery, a comms module lay on a table in an adjacent room, from which the tinny audio emanated.

"*—the family had congregated at the farm to view Niko's record-breaking match, a choice that proved fatal—*"

Niko frowned, convinced he'd misheard. The Vandes family was as safe as humanly possible, protected by security guards and with easy access to bunkers, escape vehicles, and premier doctors. His Player sponsorships ensured that.

"*—Custodians found no survivors. Investigators are looking into why the SafeShields bunker and Pureyre filtration systems both failed.*"

His frown deepened. *What the—?* Niko lurched upright, fingers twisting the blanket strewn over him. This couldn't be real. He must be having a nightmare. Or hallucinating. Maybe stress was finally getting to him. His family was safe. They *had* to be. The audio droned in the background as his vision blurred as he struggled for breath. Was he having a panic attack? Oh gods why couldn't his lungs get enough air? Why—

The reporter cut off, then a familiar voice said, "Here, drink this."

Niko blinked, gaze snapping onto Aiden approaching in long, steady strides.

The sight jostled the rest of Niko's memories: losing the game, F37 getting fogged, green eyes watching him fall down, down, down.

Those same eyes now studied him with guarded wariness, even as Aiden held out the mug in offering. "It'll help you recover faster."

A cold roar of shock pummeled through Niko, and he shot to his feet.

Alarm flashed across Aiden's face as he set the mug on the bedside drawer. "Wait—"

"No, *you* wait." Niko swayed as a swell of nausea slammed into him. He swallowed down the bile and accused, "Your day job is a Referee."

Aiden froze, then gave a terse nod. "It was."

"I . . . I would've never guessed." *How many Players*

have you executed? Would you have done the same to me, if it came down to it?

"That's kind of the whole point of being a double agent." Aiden flashed a small smile, warm and comforting, promising everything would be all right.

Except this was all wrong, everything was *not* all right. Dazed, Niko plopped down on the edge of the bed. "Can you put the news back on?"

"No, it'll only upset you."

"I need to know if my family is alive and—"

"I'm sorry for your loss." Aiden dropped his gaze for a long moment, then walked over to sit beside Niko. "They died quickly and painlessly, if that's of any comfort."

"No, no, this shouldn't have happened." Shaking his head, Niko braced his elbows on his thighs, hands laced behind his neck as he stared down at the floor. "I ensured they had everything—*everything*—to protect them from a fogging."

"Malfunctions happen. Unfortunate, but a part of life." Aiden patted Niko's back, then traced languid circles down his spine.

Niko closed his eyes, the knots in his muscle relaxing as he focused on Aiden's touch. He had to pull himself together. Collect the facts, figure out what to do next.

"It doesn't make sense," he murmured. "New SafeShields and Pureyre filters were installed recently, and the inspectors would've checked to ensure everything was up to code."

"Stop worrying over the past, Vandes. It's not going to change anything." Aiden squeezed Niko's shoulder, fingers digging into the flesh right above his collarbone.

"You're *free* now. The Games don't own you anymore. You can be with me and the Iconoclasts. Isn't this what you've always wanted? No more putting on a mask, no more being under your coach's controlling—"

"*Ivonna,*" Niko gasped. She would've been at the stadium, not on the farm.

"Don't worry, she's fine."

Niko whipped his head up, forcing Aiden's hand to slide off. "No, she's most definitely not fine. She must be absolutely distraught. Her whole family—parents, siblings, *everyone,* gone."

Sometimes Niko wondered if Ivonna loved the rest of their family more than she'd ever allowed herself to love him. He didn't blame her. Better to form a deeper attachment to people who didn't play life-or-death games for a profession. Gods, Ivonna must be devastated—he couldn't begin to fathom the pain she would be in.

"Look," Aiden sighed, "you're safe and that's all that matters. I'm sorry about the rest of the family—but Niko, they were barely more than strangers, you told me yourself. Whatever facsimile of care you held was only because your mother told you so."

"But they're still my *family.*" Ivonna's words floated off Niko's tongue, an automatic response, though guilt lingered like a ghost. Guilt that Aiden's words struck a shameful, awful truth Niko would rather ignore: he didn't—*couldn't*—care about the Vandes family the way he knew he was *supposed* to, no matter how hard he tried. He clenched his jaw, determined to fulfill the role of a dutiful son. "Family always comes first. We look out for each other."

Aiden's nostrils flared. He squared his upper body

toward Niko, then said in a low and fierce tone, "But *they're not your family,* Niko. They're just strangers who happened to share DNA with you." A pause, and then his voice gentled into a whispered plead, "Stop crying. It's freaking me out."

Niko startled, surprised when he realized the world had taken on a watery sheen.

Aiden leaned in and brushed a thumb under Niko's eye, leaving behind a burning path. "*I'm* your family. What have *they* ever done for you? Nothing except take! But I've given you freedom, truth, safety, love . . . I've given you everything you've wanted."

"Still doesn't change the fact *I* care about Ivonna." Despite his best efforts, his voice cracked. "She's hurting, Aiden. Fuck, *I'm* hurting. She seems cold and stoic on the outside, but I've also seen her laugh and cry and love. I'm her son, I should be there to comfort her. Instead, I'm fuck-knows-where and a fugitive. She must feel so betrayed."

Second-hand grief was a whole demon of its own. Life hadn't been kind to Ivonna, and he'd made it worse. She didn't deserve this. He squeezed his eyes shut, but that didn't banish the images playing across his mind: the insidious pink mist crawling over the family orchards, sinking its tentacles through the windows and cracks, permeating useless air filters.

Perhaps he'd had this coming for a long time. He'd torn apart millions of families, feeding their pieces to Karlo, and now, it was his turn to cede something to the killing fog.

"Hey, head up." Aiden pressed a knuckle beneath Niko's chin. "Focus on the future, not the past. You've been through a lot, how are you feeling, physically?"

Niko released a choked laugh then drew a deep breath. "Like absolute shit, to be honest.

Aiden made a sympathetic sound then grabbed the mug from the bedside table. "Drink. It's a recovery mixture. Electrolytes, vitamins, anti-inflammatories and a sprinkling of painkillers. Getting shocked by 250 volts is never fun—I'm sorry about that, by the way. Your body has an unusually high resistance, and it took more voltage than anticipated to knock you out."

"See? I was born to join the resistance."

That teased a quiet chuff out of Aiden. Niko dutifully swigged the citrus-flavored drink, taking comfort in Aiden's steadying presence, the warmth radiating from his skin, the familiar weight of his hand on his lap. Slowly, the physical aches and twinges dulled to a manageable hum, though internal pain slicing through his heart only sharpened. Except he didn't know what to do about it. He'd gotten his wish—escape from the Games—but at what cost?

Aiden silently took the emptied mug and walked into the adjourning room. "We're in an Iconoclast safe house, on one of the Archipelago's uninhabited islands within the National Wilderness Preserves."

After a moment, Niko followed him into the kitchen. Aside from the bedroom and kitchen, there was a bathroom to round out this simple cabin. He spotted a satellite internet multi-comms module sitting on the table and moved to pick it up.

"Don't touch that." Aiden rushed in front and powered off the module before sliding the tablet into his jacket pocket. "We need to lie low. We're both internationally-wanted fugitives. Aside from communicating with the Iconoclasts, we should avoid transmissions going in or out of here."

Niko frowned. "I could've sworn it was playing a broadcast earlier."

"Perhaps you were dreaming? You *have* been in and out of it the last three days."

"No, I'm pretty sure—I asked you to turn the news back on earlier, and you refused." Niko narrowed his eyes, noting the twitch in Aiden's cheek. He'd thought Aiden was acting unusually curt but chalked it up to stress, given the current circumstances. But blatantly lying to his face was a whole other matter altogether . . . "Why are you acting like you're hiding something?"

Aiden scoffed, but the sound came out too tight and too jagged.

Suspicion ignited in Niko. His tone hardened, sharp and pointed. An awful, terrible, impossible thought slid into his mind, and before he could help himself, he blurted, "*Did* you tamper with the SafeShields and Pureyre mechanisms?"

For a moment, it seemed Aiden was going to deny the allegation, but when Niko pinned him with a glare, he gave a stilted nod.

"Why?" Niko asked, battling back the furious wave of red threatening to swamp his vision.

He'd been willing to die for Aiden and the Iconoclasts. But what was he supposed to do when the man he would take a bullet for was the one pulling the trigger?

Aiden raked a hand through his tousled hair. Dark crescents hung beneath vivid green eyes, marking long sleepless hours. A breathy exhale rushed out of him as his shoulders slumped, the image of a hardened rebel sliding away. "I won't lie to you, Vandes, because I respect you too much for that. But yes, I gave the order to hack the farm's safeguards—don't give me that look—"

"How else am I supposed to look when I find out you murdered my family?!"

"It was for your own good."

"How so?" Niko hissed. He'd never been a violent person, but he found himself curling his hands into fists. His gaze darted around, searching for a way out lest he punched Aiden, but there was nowhere to go.

Aiden rubbed the back of his neck and glanced out the window. Conifers surrounded the small clearing they were in, with silhouettes of mountain peaks towering in the distance. He heaved another sigh. "Your mother manipulated your whole life using 'family' as an excuse—who's to say she wouldn't have used them to guilt you into returning to the Battle Team? Which wouldn't have worked, by the way, because the Iconoclasts will never let you walk out on them alive. As the only person who's ever held leverage over you, Ivonna is a threat to your safety. But I also know you valued her wellbeing, so instead of negating the threat, I got rid of the leverage."

"You don't trust me to not betray the Iconoclasts?" Niko slid Aiden a wounded expression.

"I trust you, but I don't trust others not to exploit your family to get to you."

"So you decided to exploit them yourself before someone else could."

"And if I had to, I would make the same choice all over again. The Iconoclasts wanted to postpone your induction, but the Games were killing you. I needed to get you out before it did so. If I had to choose, I would always pick sacrificing others to save you."

Niko met Aiden's sincere expression, then finally replied, "I see."

Was it sick of him to feel strangely touched by Aiden's declaration? That somebody was willing to shoulder the responsibility of picking who lived and who died, and to choose Niko when the ashes settled?

Swallowing his grief, Niko nodded and brought out *the mask*. He'd lost too much to stop, especially now that he was finally part of the rebellion. Time to double down and commit to the cause. Plus, what Aiden said was true, right? Revolution demanded sacrifices, and this was Niko's tithe. It'll be worth it at the end. That was the only acceptable outcome. He *had* to believe in it. "When do I meet the rest of the Iconoclasts?"

"Whoa, rein in your horse bot." Aiden shifted, fingers twitching as if resisting the urge to touch Niko. Instead, he thumbed through the small deck of weighted cards tucked in his jacket pocket. Niko had gifted him the trick deck after learning about Aiden's cardistry talent. The last card slipped off Aiden's thumb, and he leaned forward, gaze earnest. "You must understand, it's one thing to talk about believing in a cause, and another to *feel* it. How do you feel?"

"Like I got run over by a mag train." The smallest movements sent an unpleasant twinge through Niko's limbs. "Otherwise, I'm ready for whatever comes next."

"Eat. You need to regain your strength." Aiden pulled out a stool and maneuvered a still-perplexed Niko onto it. He ladled a bowl of oatmeal for each of them, then took the spot across from Niko. The gruel, annoyingly, smelled delicious, all cinnamon and honey. Aiden cleared his throat. "So. Here's the deal. Few people dare to be radical enough to incite change, and fewer still are in a position of power. You're a pawn to your nation's leaders, a Player to the citizens, and potential to the resistance. There's nothing quite as sweet nor powerful as potential. You're going to help us solve a mystery, Niko, and once that mystery has been solved, you're going to spread the truth to the world. As a famous Player, you have a powerful platform capable of facilitating change. But even when backed by logic and common sense, change doesn't come easy when faced against the norm. You must drag change out of the womb of dissent, kicking and screaming into this merciless world, and make what was once the norm radical, and the radical the new norm."

"Pretty speech," Niko deadpanned. "Am I supposed to clap?"

Aiden rolled his eyes. "Oh, fuck off."

Niko bit back a smirk and pointed his spoon at Aiden. "I'm already waist deep in with the Iconoclasts. No need to woo me over with moving words."

"Sorry I was just trying to hype you up for your first mission as an Iconoclast, which will start when you're feeling well enough to travel. It'll just be you and me on this assignment."

Niko lifted a wry brow. "Don't trust me to meet the others yet?"

Aiden leaned across the table then hesitated, hand hovering between them until Niko inclined his head. Something resembling relief passed across Aiden's mien as he closed the distance to tuck a piece of Niko's hair out of his face. "We're going for speed and stealth, so the less people the better. I figured you'll prefer working with someone you already know on your first assignment."

"Lucky you assumed right."

Aiden winked. "I'm always right."

"I change my mind. Can I request a new partner?" Niko twisted in his seat, mockingly searching the room. "Aiden's too arrogant for my liking."

"Hey, focus." Aiden gripped Niko's chin and turned his head forward. "Eyes on me. Listen to what I'm saying."

"Wow, bossy." Niko flicked Aiden's nose, drawing an exasperated chuckle.

"Technically, I *am* the team leader for this assignment."

"And what is the assignment?"

"I'm getting to that, if you'd stop interrupting for a second." Aiden paused, and when Niko mimed zipping his lips shut, continued. "Our task is to figure out what compounds make up Karlo. Knowing its chemical composition is the first step to developing an antidote. Once we can create an antidote, our next goal is distributing it. We've got members rooted in big pharma companies, biotech labs, chemical engineering factories, even inside Peaceful Ends—we're ready to mass produce an antidote *if* we know *how* to."

Niko loosened a whistle. "If you're able to make the antidote public, the Battle Games will lose their effectiveness."

"The whole system will collapse."

"But couldn't Peaceful Ends or some other corporation simply create a Karlo 2.0? Then we'd be back to square one."

Aiden released Niko's chin and raised a flippant shoulder. "It took them a decade to develop Karlo, even longer before it was approved for international usage. We'd have a couple years until another Karlo comes into play. That's plenty of time to rework the system."

"Into *what?*"

"Don't know, I'm sure the answer will present itself soon enough."

Niko frowned. "You should already know the end game before making your opening move. Else you're just playing blindly, and that's the fastest way to losing control of the board."

"You've left that life behind, Niko. Real life isn't a game. Shed that grimace and have trust. Isn't it enough that we're simply striving for improvement? Simply disrupting the norm by introducing a Karlo antidote will give us the opportunity to rewrite the system into something *better*."

"All right." Niko inclined his head, not entirely satisfied with the answer but eager to revert to the topic of the mission. "If you have members inside Peaceful Ends, couldn't they steal samples of Karlo to reverse engineer?"

"Peaceful Ends is the most paranoid company I've ever seen." Aiden shoveled a huge spoonful of oatmeal and spoke around his mouthful. "Their security measures are insane, and they guard Karlo like it's the secret to eternal life. Our members within the company serve as spies more than anything else. But fear not, we have members embedded within the Custodians, which is even better."

Aiden leaned back in his chair to reach a drawer and pulled out thick folder. He pushed the stack of papers over to Niko. "One of our Custodians was able to collect samples of Karlo while on the job, and our scientists broke them down to base chemicals. All the related information is in there."

He paused, shooting Niko a pointed look while polishing off his oatmeal.

Niko withheld a huff. Aiden liked his theatrics, and unfortunately, Niko was too willing to step into his casted role. He asked the silently prompted question. "Why do we need to figure out the Karlo recipe if the Iconoclasts already have it?"

"Because it's not the right recipe. We've tried creating various antidotes based on the samples our Custodian acquired, but everything failed. Eventually, the smart people determined Karlo is, for lack of a better term, a living compound. From the moment it leaves the gas canister to when it's inhaled by an unlucky soul, its chemical composition changes."

Niko thumbed through the papers and noted many of the documents were sent from a user simply referred to as *K*. "You'll want a source sample of Karlo, before it's been released into its environment. Then you can let it run its course, figure out what triggers its changes, and how you can negate them." The last page slipped off his finger as he looked up. "Why choose us for this task, though? Wouldn't someone with ties to Peaceful Ends be better?"

Aiden grabbed the emptied bowls. "Since I pulled you out early, the Iconoclasts have been scrambling to rearrange their strategy. They'd been planning for you partake in the next International Peacetime Games, but obviously that's no longer feasible. Everyone's occupied with setting up the alternative plan, so I volunteered us for this task."

Niko sauntered up behind Aiden at the sink. "All right, what's our first stop, my Fearless Leader?"

"Our Custodian gave us a little gift. Check my right jacket pocket."

Niko slipped a hand into the soft fabric and pulled out a palm-sized device. A green light blinked at one end. "What's this?"

"A jailbroken universal lock override. It'll get us into any building, vault, vehicle, you name it, without tracking each swipe or tripping any alarms for unsanctioned usage." Aiden twisted the faucet shut then turned toward Niko. "The plan is to snoop around facilities connected to Peaceful Ends."

"That could easily take us *years*. We need a strategy to pick which locations to prioritize."

"So make me a methodology, my Brilliant Strategist."

"If I were Peaceful Ends, I would minimize the transport distance between production and destination." Niko's brain raced to map the most efficient way of tackling their assignment, but Aiden's fingers caressing his lower back threatened to redirect his train of thoughts. "Production plants require a lot of water, so a location along the coast would be a good idea. The Bureau of Business posts a public list of all C-level companies and their associated addresses each year."

"Keep going, I like what I'm hearing," Aiden encouraged.

Niko hummed in appreciation. "The Marshals enforce the rules and consequences related to the Battle Games, which includes deploying Karlo. Marshals operate from Hubs . . ."

"And?"

Everything snapped into place like a plucked wire. Niko drew a sharp breath, fingers clenched tight yet shaky. "Only certain Hubs house the transportation division. It's simple—we start our search by listing all the facilities near the coast owned by Peaceful Ends. From those locations, we narrow the contenders down to those within fifty kilometer from a Hub with drone ports. This should give us a good starting point for which buildings to check first."

Niko reached for the tablet in Aiden's pocket. "Surely we can use the satellite internet to download maps and databases—"

"Nuh-uh." Aiden slapped a hand over Niko's. "Today, you rest and recover. Tomorrow, the work begins."

"But—"

"I'm the team lead. I call the shots—and I think you need to get back to full strength first."

"I'll be back to normal by tomorrow," Niko assured. "I'm capable of conducting research now."

Aiden raised a brow. "What if *I'm* not ready to start?"

He reached down to grasp Niko's hand, fingers laced, as he took a backward step toward the bedroom. "It's just you, me, and the trees out here, Vandes. No cameras. No coaches. No entities trying to control your life."

Part of Niko wanted to start on the research, another part yearned to chase after Aiden, and yet another part of him fretted over the perverse desire of wanting to *be* with Aiden. Aiden, who pulled the trigger to F37 and killed the Vandes family.

He did it for me, though. He did it for the greater good.

Plus, who was Niko to judge? He'd been a Player perpetuating an evil Game. His moral conscience was shot as it were.

"We're both fugitives." Aiden took another step, eyes beseeching. "Once we go back out there, who knows what'll happen. We could die, we could triumph, we could—"

Niko closed the distance between them in one long stride. He cupped Aiden's jaw and kissed him, tasting brown sugar and warmth. Aiden's lips curved into a smile against his own as he pulled Niko into the bedroom.

No, a revolution was not all about guts and glory. It was a bloody and sacrifice-demanding affair, something too easily romanticized in a heady rush of zeal. But just because he shouldn't romanticize a revolution didn't mean he couldn't find love in one.

GLOBAL REPORTER: SHARE YOUR THOUGHTS—NIKO VANDES, INSPIRATION OR INSURGENT?

RED ALERT: NIKO VANDES AT LARGE AND BELIEVED TO BE ARMED AND DANGEROUS—CONTACT LOCAL AUTHORITIES IMMEDIATELY IF YOU SEE HIM

GLOBAL REPORTER: CENTRAL AMERICAN ALLIANCE DEMANDS SIGNIFICANT PAYMENT FROM ATLANTIC ARCHIPELAGO NATION FOR EACH DAY NIKO VANDES REMAINS ALIVE

BREAKING NEWS: CENTRAL AMERICAN ALLIANCE ACCUSES ATLANTIC ARCHIPELAGO NATION OF HIDING AWAY PRIZED PLAYER NIKO VANDES TO ILLEGALLY TRAIN THEIR RISING STARS

BREAKING NEWS: THE INTERNATIONAL CONFLICT RESOLUTION COURT WILL FOG 1 ARCHIPELAGO SQUARE FOR EVERY DAY NIKO VANDES REMAINS ALIVE, UP TO 10 DAYS, TO MOTIVATE ARCHIPELAGO OFFICIALS TO TURN HIM IN OR INCREASE SEARCH EFFORTS

CHAPTER 7

IMANI

5 SQUARES. 402,430 HUMAN LIVES.

"What a fucking asshole," Imani muttered. "Vandes should've turned himself in five days ago if he had an ounce of decency."

"And a self-sacrificing nature," Kit commented. "Alas, most humans are predisposed to favor their survival instincts above all else." They shaded their eyes and tilted their head back, following the complex skyscrapers spiraling toward the puffy clouds. "How long do you think it took to build all this?"

She huffed, too incensed to enjoy the Fibonacci-inspired architecture of the Archipelago, so different from the glass towers of the Antarctican Republic. "Vandes is a disgrace of a Player."

"Why?" Kit challenged, zipping up the biodegradable body bags. "Because he didn't want to die?"

"He's a Player. The possibility of an early death is literally in the job description." She gestured at Kit, then herself. "Hells, a premature death is an inescapable probability for everyone. Players just have worse odds, but that's a tradeoff they accept for the luxury they live in."

Kit barked out a sharp laugh. "You think they have a choice?"

She cast them an annoyed glance. Sweat and humidity clung to her skin like a sticky web. Luckily, it'd been over seventy-two hours since this square had been fogged, so she could ditch the usual haz suit required. A whiff of burnt sugar tickled her nose, a non-lethal lingering trace of Karlo. It was the third day of her volunteer shift on the islands, and she was already looking forward to returning home. The dependability of a set routine—school, work, sleep—had eased Imani's transition into the real world after leaving the compound. As such, this abrupt departure from her usual schedule—work, cooking, sleep—had Imani's teeth on edge.

But I can't leave yet. Not until I find what I'm looking for.

If needed, she would extend her volunteer shift. When Kit had found out Imani was joining the international emergency aid crew to help the overwhelmed Archipelago Custodians, they'd decided to tag along. Though where Kit had volunteered out of the kindness of their heart, Imani had done so with an ulterior goal in mind—and she wasn't leaving until it'd been achieved.

"It's an *honor* to be a Player," Imani said. She paused to observe a pair of ducks splashing in the manmade stream winding through the city center. The Archipelago's stormwater management was a functional art form: an above ground collection system that meticulously diverted into an underground network watering the city's curated selection of native plants. Liquid roots flowing beneath the roads and buildings. "Vandes' country gave him everything he could've wanted, yet he still betrayed his people. Look at the cost of his cowardice."

She nodded down the quiet streets, at bagged bodies lining the sidewalk. "He broke the cardinal rule of the Games, and now peace has been destroyed."

Her jaw tightened, and she sped to a brisk march, as if distancing herself from the body bags dotting the roadsides like gravestones would reduce her fury.

Imani had been a Custodian for over a decade. Death didn't faze her—but this pointless slaughter over the selfish idiocy of a Player did. Society built these Players up so high they believed themselves to be gods—just like how the cultists had treated their leader like an infallible savior. When Players were forced to confront death, some simply couldn't comprehend the concept of mortality—much like how the cult had fallen into disarray when their precious savior died. Fortunately, unlike the Grand Arrival, the Games had Referees to serve as a reality check.

Except, somehow the rebels—the Iconoclasts— managed to infect both a Referee *and* a Player, violating one of the underpinning rules behind the Games: the losing Player must die. This was bad. (Very, very bad.) If one Player successfully cheated death, then it wouldn't be long before others tried to follow.

And if *that* happened, then who knew what other rules would start going out the window. A Game without rules was meaningless. A Game was *defined* by the rules that governed it.

Without rules, violence would prevail. Humanity would destroy itself. She'd experienced it firsthand, when conflict between the Grand Arrival factions couldn't be resolved.

"What's wrong?" Kit jogged up and fell in stride with Imani's clipping pace.

"Oh, just thinking about how Vandes and that rogue Referee will be the catalyst that catapults us back to the 2nd era dark ages where everything's on fire or underwater and every other country is on the verge of nuking half the population or carpet bombing the forests until everything's ash."

Kit blinked, eyes owlishly large behind the clear visor they'd opted to wear. "That's not dramatic and jumping to conclusions at all."

She shrugged. "I'm just preparing for the worst, is all."

They passed an enforcement Hub, crested a hill, and paused at the top. The road ramped down then flattened out, seemingly running straight into the ocean glittering beneath afternoon sun. To the left held the piers, colorful boats rocking in the waves. Curved buildings occupied the right, too large to be residential. The giant recirculation pipes flowing down their sides into the sea left no question that these were industrial.

"Life as we know it is at risk of being overturned," Imani murmured, hands on her hips as she surveyed the land below. "Peace shattered. Chaos reigning. Normalcy nonexistent." She turned and locked eyes with Kit. "Societal balance will be overturned if more Battle Game rules are broken."

"Uh-huh," Kit responded, dubious.

She scowled. They didn't see the dark future they were hurtling toward unless the scales of justice were restored to equilibrium. "Forget it, you wouldn't understand, not unless you've witnessed the base violence humans will resort to if left unbridled."

Kit's expression softened. Unlike Oran, Kit knew about Imani's childhood.

She clenched Ulo in one gloved hand, daring them to *pity* her. "I didn't survive 72 hours hiding in a closet, wondering if a stray bullet would kill me before I died of thirst, for some selfish Player to ruin my life because they think *their* life is more important than mine—more important than anyone else's."

"No, of course not," Kit murmured. "But don't confuse the past for the present. If you continue revisiting the past, you'll soon find yourself reliving it."

To that, she had no response. Her fingers tightened around Ulo even more as she marched down the hill and toward the sprawling industrial buildings. She walked past a hospital's front doors. Not even patients on life support and oxygen tanks escaped Karlo's grasp—the city's power shut down when the countdown hit zero, unplugging their lives as well.

"Hey, where are you going?" Kit's leggy strides easily caught up. "We're supposed to be clearing the financial district—"

"Return to the group. There's something else I need to do."

Empty condos stared back at her, their residents gently, violently vacated. Two crows hopped down the road before startled into flight.

To her annoyance, Kit didn't listen. (Of course they didn't. They were *Kit.)*

"What are you doing?" they pressed.

"Capturing Niko Vandes and turning him in."

Kit skidded to a halt and yanked on her arm. "Um, I don't often say this so the fact I am should mean something—but *I don't think that's a good idea.*"

She shook them off with an annoyed glower, resuming her advancement to the coast. "Pot calling the pan black."

"Kettle."

"Never asked for your opinion."

They flapped their arms like a disgruntled seagull. "Niko is dangerous! He runs with the Iconoclasts, who *bombed* three enforcement Hubs just this week. He won't hesitate to kill you. Plus, what makes you think he's even here? He's likely fled the Archipelago."

A smirk curled across Imani's face. "Oh, he's somewhere here all right."

The past week had been filled with sleepless nights hunting down Vandes' whereabouts. Like a spider gathering information based on the vibrations from different parts of its web, Imani had plucked at the various strands of her network. Thirteen years as a Custodian had enabled her to gather an impressive collection of connections with other Custodians, Referees, Marshals, and employees that played sideline role in the Games. By asking an unassuming question here and requesting a small favor there, she'd unearthed enough dirt on Niko Vandes to bury him.

She learned Niko came from a small city in the northern regions of the Archipelago, that he could deal a mean deck of cards, and that he enjoyed sharing drinks with Aiden Tays at Bar None. All her research led here, to the Archipelago coast. The last place one would expect to find an escaped fugitive is back in enemy territory.

"Imani," Kit nearly tripped over their own feet walking backward to face her unrelenting march, "leave this to the professionals. The Marshals will find Vandes sooner or later."

She snorted and picked up her pace, forcing them to side step. "It'll be later at this rate. *Five squares,* Kit. That's how many squares have been unnecessarily fogged." Her voice sharpened. "So either you come with me and stop complaining, or leave."

They sighed and nodded. "Friends stick together."

Friends? Is that what they were? She supposed Kit was the closest person she had to a friend. They were certainly closer to her than any other coworkers. Warmth bloomed under her sternum at the idea of her and Kit being friends. Someone she could rely on.

"Okay, what's the plan?" Kit asked once they reached the street filled with industrial buildings.

"These four are owned by Peaceful Ends." Imani pointed at the adjacent structures. "Two of them are research laboratories for experimental drugs that enhance mental focus, stamina, and processing speed, among other things. Two are manufacturing sites for on-the-market pharmaceuticals. You take the labs and I'll take the manufacturing plants. If one of us finds Vandes, alert the other with our emergency beacon."

"We shouldn't split up."

"It'll be faster if we do. The sooner we find Vandes,

the fewer lives lost."

"Fine, then let's search the same building but take different floors," Kit proposed. "This way, we can reach each other faster if needed."

She considered the suggestion, then acquiesced. "Is your Ulo fully charged?"

They shouldn't need the gadget since all locks should've disengaged when Karlo was released, but sometimes glitches happened.

Kit pulled a face and held up their own universal lock override device. "You know it's weird that you've named it, right?"

"You know the tomato-and-chicken sandwich you have for lunch every day is the saddest excuse of a meal, right?" she shot back. (Seriously, the sandwich had no seasoning or sauce or anything. Even back at the compound there was at least a steady supply of dried onion and garlic salt.)

They laughed and pocketed the gadget. "Not everyone can be a gourmet cook like you. What's the plan after spotting Vandes and notifying each other? Confront him? Follow him?" Alarm spiked Kit's voice as they scanned over Imani. "You don't have a gun, do you? You're not going to *kill* him, right?"

"No, no," she soothed and opened the main door of the manufacturing plant. "If you find him, call for the Marshals. We'll let them handle the rest."

They nodded, relief relaxing their features.

She gestured through the entryway. "After you. You start from the top floor and I'll start from the bottom. Keep comms open on the private channel."

They nodded and parted ways.

The motion-activated lights turned on as Imani breezed through the corridor into the stairwell. Her boots echoed against the steps as she descended into the twilight zone of the building. Finally, after traveling at least six stories underground, she hit the lowest level.

The walls and shadows stretched over her, oppressive and ominous. According to an emergency evacuation map, a dozen small rooms occupied most of this level, with two larger ones at either end. Sweat dripped into her eyes as she strode for the largest room.

Imani reached the door at the end of the hallway. It was limned in the soft red glow of the emergency exit arrow.

She pushed on the door, but it didn't budge. Strange.

Ah, of course. It's a pull door.

She gripped the handle and gave it a yank, but still the door didn't move, and now she was fairly convinced she could hear the hum of a mag-lock powered on. Her heart raced. Sweat pooled in her palms. Someone had re-engaged the lock after the initial EMP blast.

Someone had been here recently.

Glancing over her shoulder to confirm nobody had snuck up, Imani turned on Ulo and was about to use it to force open the door when it swung wide.

She startled and stifled a gasp. Niko Vandes stared back at her.

CHAPTER 8
NIKO

AN HOUR EARLIER

I T'D BEEN THREE DAYS SINCE NIKO AND AIDEN took the solar rover and left the cabin, and a week since their grand escape from Paxania Stadium. Upon returning to the urban sprawl of the Archipelago mainlands, Niko had been horrified to learn several squares had been fogged in their absence.

Why? Niko had whispered as they'd threaded through a silent city like wraiths, taking advantage of the unlocked buildings to investigate the addresses on their search list.

To send a message, Aiden replied grimly. *Resist the Games, and even more will die. Fear is a powerful weapon.*

Did my actions at the last Game trigger the fogging? Niko wondered with a sinking feeling. Hadn't sacrificing his family been enough? How much of a higher price would the revolution demand? *Could* it even demand more?

Aiden had laid a hand on Niko's shoulder, warm

fingers brushing across his nape. *No, Niko. This mass fogging has been a long time coming. It's not your fault.*

Niko had gulped and accepted the offered reassurance, even if he couldn't quite wash away the taste of lies lingering on his tongue. Which only made the guilt sit ever heavier in his stomach.

They still didn't have access to the most current news—Aiden insisted remaining a low profile was even more important now that they were no longer hundreds of kilometers from civilization. So they depended on whatever updates Aiden received through his secure channel with the Iconoclasts.

Now, combing through their seventh building—a research laboratory and small-scale manufacturing plant for experimental products—the hopeful flame that'd been kindled in the cabin was dwindling. Promising trails had led to dead ends. Not to mention the staggering death tolls they'd encountered had cast an iron mantle over Niko's shoulders.

"It hits different when it's in person compared to a number on the screen," he murmured as they jogged down the stairwell to the basement level of the facility. He'd known his victories came at a steep cost, but there'd always been a buffer between him and reality. "The bunker we passed earlier was the worst . . ."

He shivered. Aiden made a sympathetic sound.

The images pressed against the back of Niko's eyes: several hundred bodies fallen around the emergency shelter, all of them so close to salvation yet mere seconds too late from being saved. They'd been on their way back to the makeshift base camp, darting behind vehicles as cover, when Niko had paused to watch Custodians finish bagging the victims and open the bunker doors. The wails of families discovering their loved ones hadn't survived still echoed in Niko's ears. And to think this terrible scene had played out over and over every time he won a Battle Game, had played out at the Vandes family farm when Ivonna found out—

He inhaled a sharp breath. All the more reason to end the Games.

"There must be tons of people protesting using Karlo outside of the Games," Niko said. "I mean, how can anyone think this is acceptable?"

"That's why we need to focus on the mission." Aiden opened the door at the end of the corridor, waited for Niko to pass through, then locked it. "The sooner we can roll out an antidote, the sooner this terrible nonsense can stop."

The lights clicked on automatically, but Niko shut them off in favor of a flashlight. He shone the beam across the long room. The first half of the room contained rows of lab tables. Tall shelving stacks occupied the back half, shadowy giants ensconced in darkness.

"Over there." Niko pointed his light at the data banks and monitors.

While Aiden worked on breaching the security system with their jailbroken universal lock override, Niko perused the rest of the room. A walk-in fridge with a keypad on it. A bunch of bulletproof-and-radiation proof safes. A treasure trove of high-end tech lying on open shelving, like fruits at the market waiting to be grabbed.

"Target hit!" Aiden crowed, leaning toward the monitor, the blue wash of pixels sharpening the contours of his cheeks. He stepped aside for Niko to view the screen. "Does this look right to you?"

He'd pulled up an encrypted folder titled *Project Sweet Dreams*. Inside were files containing logs dating back fifty years ago, showing iterations of the drug codenamed Sweet Dreams. The last note in the file stated *Approved and chosen by the International Conflict Resolution Court. Phase III of Project Sweet Dreams: Complete. Next Phase: Public release.*

"Target found," Niko confirmed. "That was surprisingly . . ."

Easy died on his tongue. He'd expected needing to dig harder, crack some sort of riddle or kidnap a Peaceful Ends employee to acquire the Karlo recipe. Sneaking into an empty building and hacking a computer felt anticlimactic.

He shook his head, rueful at himself. *The Player in you is showing, Vandes.* Not everything had to be done with pomp and fanfare. Impactful events could happen quietly.

"The world ends not with a bang, but a whimper," Niko murmured.

"Hey, we did it." Aiden nudged him with an elbow. "You could act a little less melancholic about it. The world's not ending, it's being reborn."

Niko answered with a feeble smile and pulled out two memory chips from his pocket. Aiden took the tiny metal squares, dexterous fingers slotting them into the computer to copy over the files. He had the fingers of a cardist—quick and precise. The thought of Aiden coaxing cards into hypnotizing patterns and flourishes made Niko smile.

"Our first successful mission, with many more to come," Aiden proclaimed as the progress bar popped onto the screen. Ten minutes remaining. "I'm taking you back to the Iconoclast headquarters after this. It's not easy to access, but the leaders want to meet you in person."

"Where is it, on the moon?" Niko laughed.

"It might as well be," Aiden answered seriously. "Usually it takes at least a week's notice to plan a visit."

Niko's eyes widened. "Wait, where *is* it?"

"Not where, but *what*. It's a submersible mobile platform." Aiden smirked at Niko's shock. "It houses about fifty members full time and can support another hundred or so guests passing through. The headquarters is a salvaged maritime support hub from World War IV updated with stealth tech and an advanced hospital ward. The platform's mobility provides better support for hotbeds of Iconoclast activity and reduces its likelihood of being detected compared to a static location."

"Now I really want to go."

"Don't worry, you will. I'm very keen on introducing you to the best sushi you've ever eaten. Straight from the sea, as fresh as it gets." Aiden drew a deep breath, his joviality morphing into earnestness. "And I would like to introduce you to the other Iconoclasts as my boyfriend."

Niko stared for a beat. "Aiden Tays, are you asking me out?"

Aiden flashed his bashful-yet-confident grin that was Niko's particular brand of weakness. "Maybe?"

"Do the others know about me?"

"I mean, obviously they've heard of you. You're famous."

Niko's gaze flicked to the progress bar—eight minutes left—then back to Aiden. "What *was* I to you, then? Friend with benefits? A useful pawn for the Iconoclasts that you also happened to fu—"

"I didn't know you would follow through and join for sure." Aiden grazed his knuckles under Niko's chin once, softly, before dropping his hand. "But now that you have . . . Niko, will you be my boyfriend?"

Aiden didn't deny Niko had been a pawn. But Niko was also a fool with his heart balancing on a knife's point. He didn't mind being a pawn so long as his player was Aiden. At least, that's what Niko told himself, and not because Aiden had effectively cut him off from any other alternatives—Ivonna wouldn't help a son she no doubt blamed for the deaths of her family, and any friends or allies Niko might've had would turn him over to the law.

The estimated time ticked down to seven minutes.

Niko swallowed thickly. Who cared if he had no option but to stay with Aiden? This was what Niko wanted in the first place, anyway, to be with Aiden and the Iconoclasts. This is what he would've chosen if he had a choice.

He stepped close and brushed his lips by Aiden's ear. "Let's finish this mission, then you can take me on a proper first date and we can talk."

Aiden turned to press a quick kiss onto the corner of Niko's mouth. "Deal."

Anticipation fluttered against Niko's ribs, but he clipped them down, focusing on the task at hand. He pointed toward the back of the room. "The walk-in fridge might have Karlo samples, and I saw at least two portable cryogenic cases we can use for transport. Since you know what the Iconoclasts need more than me, why don't you grab what they might need while I keep watch on the data copying?"

Aiden nodded and set off into the maze of dark shelves.

Alone, the silence pressed against Niko as he stared at the screen, watching the progress bar creep toward the finish line. He dragged a stool over and perched on it.

A soft *thud* indicated Aiden had accessed the cold storage. Half a minute later, his low voice carried over. "They've got hundreds of Karlo samples!"

"Take as much as you can." Niko aimed his flashlight at the ceiling and spun on the stool, watching the circular beam rotate, faster and faster until it became a blurry streak. Things were finally coming together—escaping the Games, embarking on the next chapter with Aiden, finding the recipe for Karlo, and now getting actual samples of the fog.

Aiden said, "It's going to take time to load all the vials into the carrier."

"I'll help as soon as the files finish copying. There are a few minutes left."

"Sounds good."

The fridge door shut, blocking out the sounds of Aiden rummaging from within.

A couple seconds later, two loud thumps sounded from the door leading out into the corridor. Niko hooked his ankles around the stool's foot bar to cease the spinning, gaze narrowing in on the door handle as an unmistakable metallic jangling rang out. Someone was messing with the lock.

He hopped off the stool and glanced around. Should he hide or barricade the door?

On the monitor, the progress bar hit 100%. The files had successfully copied over to both memory chips, and Niko removed them from the computer as the mysterious visitor continued messing with the door handle. He didn't dare shout for Aiden and give away their presence to whoever was outside. Perhaps they might give up and leave.

A loud *clunk* rang out followed by a series of clicks as the lock disengaged. Or not. He sighed and stepped up to the door.

Coach Ivonna's Rule #4: Always control the first move.

He hoped Game rules were also applicable to real life as he disengaged the lock and yanked on the handle.

The door swung open and triggered the sensors. Overhead lights snapped on, blinding and jarring. When his vision finally refocused, Niko found himself staring at a short woman with an expression akin to a pissed-off alley cat.

CHAPTER 9
IMANI

█ MANI CLICKED ON HER COMMS TO CONTACT
Kit, but static buzzed in her earpiece. When she tried again, an automated voice chirped, *"No reception found."*

Shit, this wasn't good.

Somehow, her brain had skipped over *how* she would capture Niko, and fast-forwarded to her triumphantly handing him over to the Marshals.

Niko stared back at her with his trademark Game face, betraying not an ounce of surprise. "Hello, there."

She blinked. *That* was the first thing a champion-Player-turned-fugitive wanted to say? Squinting, she moved inside the room and shut the door, blocking off the only visible escape route.

The good news: Niko didn't seem to be armed.

The bad news: Imani also wasn't armed and had no idea how to get Niko to do what she wanted him to do—which was peacefully going to the Marshals (while also feeling ashamed for his actions).

So she decided to do the next thing she *did* know how to do, which was giving him a piece of her mind.

"You really are something, Niko Vandes," she growled. "You're an ungrateful bastard who thinks himself better than everyone else, when that mindset proves you're *worse.* You're a traitor who turned your back on the country that gave you everything you could've asked for, in favor of running with dissenters determined to dissolve world peace. You think you're so clever, but you simply mask your inadequacy with fake grins and false confidence."

She paused to draw a breath and he snatched the chance to ask, "Are you done?"

"No." She glared at his smugly stoic face. "I hope you rot in the respective hell of every religious domination. Do you even care about 402,430 lives that have been taken because *you* refuse to turn yourself in?"

The corners of his brown eyes tightened a fraction, the first fissure in his mask. "Wait, what?"

"Playing dumb won't fool me." She jabbed a finger in his face. "It's day fucking five, and each day you allow a square to be fogged proves you're truly the asshole who thinks his life is worth more than a million others."

The fissure of emotion spread, genuine distress rippling across his face.

No, don't fall for it. This is an act. He was a trained Player and could smile at her face while stabbing her in the back.

"What do you mean it's day five?" he asked. "And how did *I* allow the fogging to happen? That's the exact opposite of what I want."

Her conviction wavered at his apparent confusion,

which seemed too real to be a lie. Surely it couldn't hurt if she replied, "Your escape has set off the international turmoil of the decade. The Battle Court has allowed the Central American Alliance to fog an Archipelago square for each day you remain missing, up to ten days."

His face paled as he staggered backward.

"402,430 people have been killed in the past five days because of *you*," she said, enjoying a perverted glee at his horrified disbelief. It was good to remind the Players that they were vulnerable to guilt, too. Remind them they were mortals, not gods.

"I didn't know," he croaked, then pinned her with a piercing stare. "Wait, how do I know you're not lying?"

"Look at the news. That's all anyone is talking about."

He cursed. "Bleeding hells . . . I didn't know, I didn't have access to the news . . . 2,314,624 lives."

The last part was whispered so low Imani wouldn't have heard if she hadn't been watching his lips. She sneered in disgust. "Are those the additional lives you've taken since joining the Iconoclasts?"

He shook his head and released a heavy sigh, glancing at the door behind Imani yet making no move to escape. Like a Player who had lost a match and accepted their fate of thirty amps straight to the heart.

For an Iconoclast rebel, he was surprisingly placid. She'd expected fighting. Shouting. Bloodshed. That sort of uncouth behavior. A peaceful revolution seemed too oxymoronic to be true.

"1,912,194 is the number of lives I took as a Player. Combined with the 402,430, that's 2,314,624 lives." Apparently Niko was also a human calculator. A glint glimmered in his eyes, matching his daggered tone. "Does that make me a worse person than what you already think of me?"

"Lives lost from an actual Battle Game don't count."

"Really, now?"

She raised her chin and firmed her voice. Those hours of debate with Kit were finally paying off, because she had an armory of counterarguments ready to fire off. "Those lives were different. Those lives were taken in accordance with a set of rules to maintain peace and order. The lives taken because of *you* were taken out of—"

"Those millions of lives were taken as collateral," Niko interjected venomously. *"Collateral."*

"Not collateral, but a *necessary cost.*" She gnashed her teeth. He was being obstinate and he knew it. "Everyone *agreed* to the Battle Games Accord. Those lives were taken consensually."

"I don't remember signing my name on the Battle Games Accord. Hells, I wasn't even born yet."

She waved a hand and scoffed. "I'm sure you signed something along the lines of agreement when you joined the Archipelago Battle Team."

A flash of sorrow flickered across his face so quickly Imani reckoned she imagined it. "Actually, I didn't," he murmured. "One day I was living with my family in F37, and the next day three Marshals escorted me out of the house and to the academy. I was four."

A beat of silence dragged by. Imani ignored the twinge in her chest at the personal tidbit of information. Niko was a Player. He was trying to play her emotions to throw her off guard.

Straightening her spine and steeling her voice, she stated, "Obviously not every single person can physically sign the Battle Games Accord, but the majority of the populace agrees with its terms. The Games are the best way to resolve international conflict while still capturing the price of war."

His eyes sharpened, judging. "Thus implying war is paid with human lives."

"Hasn't it always been? *That's* the price of war. Money and lives. Nothing else compares, nothing else carries the same weight. Battle Games allow everything to be concluded civilly while satisfying the demands of war. Prisoners and mass starvation and poisoned lands and the brutality of wars past are no more. Without resorting to historical warfare, how else can conflicts be resolved when all other means have been exhausted? When talks at the table yield no results? Because here's the truth: talk is cheap. When two players can't agree, there must be a winner and loser. Not everyone can be a winner, so we *need* the Games to determine who wins and who loses."

"Talk is only cheap when it comes from liars," Niko commented. "Maybe we have the wrong people sitting on the councils."

"You speak traitorous words."

"Well, you *did* call me a traitor earlier. Regardless, thank you for sharing your thoughts." He dipped his head in a facsimile of politeness. "If you don't mind, I've got places to be."

She curled her lip and advanced a step. "You're not going anywhere. I've already called in enforcement and the Marshals will be here any second."

He raised a lazy brow. "There's no comms reception down here."

Dammit. Time to improvise Plan B. Hopefully Kit would realize something had gone awry when they didn't hear from her soon.

Niko and Imani both shifted, mirroring each other's steps, stuck at an impasse. They stared each other down. Imani blocking the door, Niko looking very reluctant to throw the first punch. In fact, Imani was seriously considering treating him to a well-aimed right hook (she went through a brief boxing phase) when a thought struck her. Niko was part of the Iconoclast *organization*—so where was the rest of his team? Was he stalling for time to be rescued or—

As if reading her thoughts, Niko cut her a dust-dry smile. "Yes, I'm stalling, but not for the reasons you think. I'm buying time for my partner to escape. Since I'm presuming you primarily care about turning me in, surely you can't object to that."

She shivered. Was she so easy to read, as transparent as crystalline ice?

He abruptly raised both hands and said, "If you think the Games can solve everything, then let's play one."

She gaped, then crossed her arms, ready to call off his ludicrous suggestion. She was a Custodian. The idea of someone like her partaking in a Game was akin to a gardener jumping into the cockpit. Plus, the Games were reserved for important issues. Stuff that affected millions of people, not two.

"Here are the stakes," he continued, because what was a game if not a competition of stakes? "If I win, I walk away free. You won't try to stop me, and you won't call law enforcement on me. If you win, I'll peacefully go with you to whatever authorities you want."

Imani pressed her lips together and sucked in her cheeks. If Niko remained on the loose, his mere existence would affect millions of citizens. Perhaps this wasn't the worst idea . . .

Yet, if *she* lost and Niko walked free, then the lives consumed by the next fogged square would be on her. Her stomach clenched at the thought. She held the power of capturing Niko Vandes—or killing off hundreds of thousands more.

It's not murder if it's part of the Game. Then it was a social contract, even if this wasn't an official Battle Game.

"It seems like a stacked match," she hedged. "A professional Player versus a Custodian. The Games are supposed to be *fair.*"

"Let's make one up, then." He gestured around. "We'll use whatever items available for game pieces and set the rules together. This way, no one has any advantage."

Imani shook her head, still unconvinced. Plus, the pit in her stomach remained a yawning chasm at the possibility of dooming all those lives. Fuck, did Players carry this dreadful weight every time they stepped up to the board? To know they would either be venerated or vilified, depending on how they played; to walk into the arena as a Player, and leave as either a savior or slayer.

She cleared her throat. "*I'll* follow the rules and honor the stakes. But will *you?* You've proven willing to cheat."

The corners of his lips twisted. "The line between *cleverness* and *cheating* is as gray as it is blurry. Anyway, you really believe the Referees would allow cheating during a Game? They've got their anti-cheating system locked down tight."

"You cheated death with that last Battle Game. You weren't being clever, just selfish."

"Not if the game I was playing is *survival*."

"Sounds like an excuse."

He held out a hand. A metal square lay flat on his palm, gleaming near-white beneath the harsh fluorescent light, reminiscent of a white flag.

"I recorded instructions for making Karlo on this card. The Iconoclasts want this to develop an antidote."

She jerked back at the revelation. "You . . . you can't do that. If people get ahold of antidotes, that would overturn the effectiveness of the Games and society will revert back to the savagery that nearly wiped out humanity and annihilated Earth. Trust me on that."

"But you could prevent that from happening if you win this game." Niko grabbed her wrist and dropped the memory card into her palm before folding her fingers over it. "My mission success depends on this card making its way to the Iconoclasts. Take it as a token of my word. I trust you to return it should I win."

She nodded and pocketed the tiny piece of metal. Even if she lost, she planned on breaking the card instead of giving it back to Niko. It was too risky to leave intact.

Cheater, a voice accused in the back of her mind.

This doesn't count, she retorted. *We're not arguing over political conflict. I'm trying to preserve society as we know it.*

He stuck out a hand, waiting for her to shake. "What's your name?"

"Imani Tenzing."

"Ready? This is what you wanted. Playing a game to settle our disagreement."

She stared at his slender fingers and slowly uncurled her own.

He flashed her a bleak grin. "Unless you're having second thoughts. Playing is completely different from spectating, isn't it? Suddenly it seems equally absurd and terrifying that every choice you make will irrevocably affect others."

Niko leaned in, lowering his voice to a dark and dangerous whisper. "Play, Imani. Or walk away and forget our meeting here ever happened. You've reaped the benefits of a stable society at the expense of others. I don't blame you—it's only human nature to accept the status quo, especially when it favors you. So willing to ignore the truth as long as it doesn't shatter your version of reality."

She flinched as a deep-buried memory unearthed itself.

Imani was eight-years-old, cleaning water filters with her father. *But what if there is no Grand Arrival coming to save us?*

Don't speak such nonsense, he had rebuked, unable to accept a reality in which a divine rapture does not exist.

But what if—

There will be, her father said in a tone that ended discussion.

Imani swallowed hard and ignored the edges Niko's words cut into her. She seized his hand and shook twice. "Let's play."

THERE WAS A CERTAIN POETIC JUSTICE IN Niko's suggestion to play a game to determine his fate. Finally, those who initiated the game would also be paying the price. A shot of surety blazed down his spine as he straightened his stance, chin lifting with newfound determination.

Niko, you have a Game scheduled tonight. Friendly match, low stakes.

Niko, you will be competing in the Southwest International Junior Battle Games League in three days as the youngest Player in its history.

Niko, you've been called to the board. A Battle Game with Eastern Australia.

Always *Niko play this* or *Niko play that*. Always getting ordered to play and risk his own life.

But this game was one *he* chose to play.

"Let's collect material to use as game pieces and meet back here in five minutes," he suggested, hoping this would give him time to find Aiden.

Unfortunately, Imani pointed to a lab table with

an assortment of supplies already scattered across it. "We can use those."

"A roll of graph paper, two digi-binders, three sheets of holographic sticker labels, five pens, a paperweight, and a stylus," Niko listed off the items as they walked over to the table.

He beelined for the side where he faced into the room, and Imani took the opposite end with her back toward the walk-in fridge.

Control the board.

Niko already knew he was going to win, though he was careful with phrasing his words to give Imani belief she had a shot at victory. The short woman patted the pocket she'd tucked the memory chip in, then unrolled the graph paper.

Control the board.

He knew there was a chance Imani wouldn't return the chip even if he won, so of course he had precautions in place, such as concealing the second memory card in his hidden jacket pocket.

"Every good game should have an objective, allowances, and restrictions," he said. "What's the objective here?"

Imani pressed her fingertips against the thin bamboo paper, each grid reminiscent of the latticed map that would flash on the display screens in Paxania Stadium. "There's a naval strategy game that became popular prior to the Second World War where players tried to sink each other's enemy ships."

"Part strategy, part luck." Niko knew the game she meant. "Just like the games played nowadays. You want to make our own version of that battleship game?"

"Something like that." She ripped the graph paper into three equal sheets, then passed one piece to him along with a digi-binder. "Use the binder to hide your map."

He stared down at his sheet of paper which apparently represented a map. "That's a lot of ocean."

She ignored his comment and tossed over a pen. "Draw out your country, sticking to the grid outline. You can make up the landform shape."

He clicked the pen. "What's the catch?"

"Each of our country has a population of ten million people, evenly distributed. So if your country has ten squares, then each square contains a million citizens. Game's over when you lose more than half of your population."

Niko propped up the binder to hide his map. The most strategic setup would be to shade out a handful of individual squares, like archipelago islands scattered across—

"And the number of squares your country must contain is dictated by the last two digits on your binder identification number," Imani finished.

She held up her binder and pointed to the stamped 571232 at the bottom of the spine before propping it upright to shield her paper. "For example, my country has to occupy thirty-two squares, so I'll go ahead and shade thirty-two squares in a pattern of my choosing."

Niko leaned over to peer at his own binder, reading the digits upside down. "Seventeen for me. Do the squares need to be connected or can they be islands?"

"Trying to form your own Archipelago, I see."

"No, just trying to be strategic."

She pursed her lips for a beat then decided, "The first number on your binder dictates how many independent land masses you can have."

Niko checked his and grimaced—a 1. "Maybe I shouldn't have asked for clarification. Can't break the rules if they don't exist."

Imani glanced at his binder and clicked her tongue. "Unfortunate. I didn't check your number ahead of time, by the way. In case you suspected I was trying to give myself an unfair advantage."

"Never thought that. You're not the type to cheat."

"Right. I mean, what are the chances that your number would begin with a 1?"

"It's all about chance and control," he sang, drawing a surprised laugh from her.

"I thought your motto was *Control the board?*"

"*Control the board but chance could still screw it up* doesn't inspire nearly as much confidence. There's only so much a Player can control on the game board—the rest is up to chance." He paused and caught her eye. "So knowing that there is some form of chance involved with every Game, do you still think leaving the fate of nations in the hands of luck to be the right thing to do?"

She glared, and if she weren't holding the pen, he imagined she would've had her hands on her hips. "I'm not interested in your preaching."

"I wasn't preaching, I was asking a question."

She tapped the top of her binder. "Focus on the game, Vandes."

"Evading my question seems to indicate that *maybe* you don't want to admit I have a valid point." He grinned at her glower. "Okay, *okay*. If I understand correctly, our goal is to 'fog' each other until we wipe out half of one person's population. Do we call out locations to fog based on a Cartesian coordinate system?"

She nodded.

Twirling the pen between his fingers as he debated the best way to draw out his imaginary nation, he mused, "Like how the method through which war is conducted has evolved over the course of centuries, so has this time-proven classic of a game. It's too bad those who ultimately suffer the greatest from warfare has not changed. Always the wealthy waging war and the poor paying the price."

Imani clicked her pen a couple times then started sketching on her own paper, pausing only to glare over the top of her binder. "If you're so quick to bash the Battle Games, what's your proposed alternative? You got a better solution?"

"Well, it's a complex issue to address." He pressed the pen nib onto the paper, watching ink bleed into a blurry border, then started forming his country. "It's a multistep process, not a simple flip of the switch."

"Fine. Then what's the first step? The second step?"

He finished marking out his landmass. "Step one is making sure Karlo can't be used to hurt people anymore."

"What if they replace Karlo with something even worse?"

"Ha! You've implied Karlo *is* bad."

She scoffed and rolled her neck, joints popping like voltage arcs. "A *necessary* bad. The least bad of many bad options."

"But still *bad,* nonetheless. How can we accept

something as it is when we know it's *not good?* The worst choice is letting it fester, unchanged." He splayed his hands in self surrender. "I don't have all the answers, but what I *do* know is we can always do better. We should always *try* to do better. If we don't, then that'll be the end of humanity. Complacency is the death of progress, no?"

"I said to stop preaching," Imani snapped, but her words carried no heat.

Niko bit the inside of his cheek. Imani was slowly but surely softening her stance on the infallibility of the Battle Games. Done with marking out his map, he raked his gaze across the pieces, shifting back into game mode. His mind filtered out all distractions as he mentally reviewed the rules, poking and prodding to find how he might bend and twist them. When he joined the Iconoclasts, he'd made a promise to walk away from the board. Yet here he was. Ready for one last game.

"First move to you." He tipped his head toward Imani.

She replied with a solemn nod, and the game commenced.

CHAPTER 11

IMANI

MANI ONLY NEEDED TO FIND ONE MORE OF Niko's squares, and then victory would be hers. Excitement buzzed down her arms as she called her next coordinate set. "13, 23."

"Miss." Niko leaned over to mark the "fogged" square on the world map between them.

"Did the Iconoclasts recruit you?" Imani blurted the question that'd been nagging her. "Or did you reach out to them?"

He paused for a moment, finished crossing off the grid, then settled back on his side of the table. "Does it matter? The Iconoclasts didn't blackmail or brainwash me. Stop trying to pin the blame on them. 15, 23."

"Miss." She fiddled with Ulo under the table, fingers grazing over familiar indentations and ridges on the gadget. "I'm having trouble reconciling this," she nodded at Niko, so composed and cool headed despite losing by a significant margin, "with anarchists. Why the hells are you siding with the Iconoclasts when they're trying to incite pandemonium? Even you admitted earlier you didn't know exactly *how* the Battle Game should evolve, only that it needed to. But causing chaos won't help anyone."

She pressed Ulo against the locked cabinet under the table. Once the device was securely stuck to the drawer's side, she quickly marked off the corresponding square on the world map.

"The Iconoclasts are trying to incite change, not chaos," Niko said with absolute certainty. Either he wasn't telling her everything about the organization, or he'd truly drank the punch.

Imani wanted to believe in the former. As far as her first face-to-face interaction with Niko went, he seemed like a rational and sharp-minded young adult. Nothing suggested him to be crazy enough to join an evil cult. Well, nothing except for faking his own death, escaping the Referees, breaking into secure facilities and who knows how many other laws . . . which wasn't too far off from what *she'd* done to figure out Niko's whereabouts. She'd excused her own lawbreaking in the name of the greater good, but then again, so had Niko. Fuck, were they *both* delusional?

She swallowed hard and rested a finger against Ulo's "unlock" button, ready to break one more law. This was the right thing to do. Sometimes you had to break a few rules to reinforce the right ones.

Niko continued. "The best way to incite change is when the norm has been destabilized. *That's* what the Iconoclasts are doing right now: making room for change."

"Hm." She ran his words through her brain, hating how his stupid, traitorous words dared to make any sort of sense.

"30, 23."

"Miss. 30, 23."

His eyes darted over her shoulder before dropping down to the center board.

"Hit," Imani determined.

He gave a stiff nod.

She pressed the "unlock" button on Ulo. In the lower frays of her vision, a red warning light blinked on. She'd never used Ulo for non-sanctioned purposes before. Didn't want dwell on the consequences of doing so.

She clicked the button again, overriding the warning. Under the table, Ulo's red light steadied into one, continuous emittance, signaling the internal safeguard had been triggered. Perfect. Ulo's signal was powerful enough to get past the walls, informing law enforcement of their current location. She'd been banking on the device's emergency broadcast to have a stronger signal than her comms piece.

Cheater. Liar. A chorus sang in her skull. *Hypocrite. You haven't won, yet you're already calling for his arrest.*

Imani licked her lips, swiping away the bitter taste of guilt. She couldn't in good conscience let Niko walk away, knowing each day of his freedom cost countless lives.

Still doesn't change the fact you're a liar-cheater-hypocrite.

"Are you going to mark off the square?" Imani asked, raising her voice to banish the whispers. She jutted her chin at the world map.

Niko dragged his gaze back to the table. Was there

something behind her that had gotten his attention? Imani debated turning around to check, but didn't dare take her eyes off Niko in case it was a ploy to distract.

She hawk-eyed Niko's nimble fingers as he crossed off the square, then startled when he abruptly flipped down his folder, revealing his hidden map.

He flashed her a smile that read more like a grimace. "Congratulations. You win."

She breathed out a relieved sigh. *Ha, see? I'm not a cheater by summoning law enforcement!*

You didn't know you were going to win, the whispers argued back.

Who cares if I celebrated my victory a little early?

Last minute comebacks aren't unheard of.

Oh, shut up! She squeezed her eyes shut. Ugh, she was sleep-deprived. She couldn't wait to hand Niko over to the authorities. Then she could go back to her normal life and go to bed at a normal hour and get some rest like a normal person. *Normalcy.* That's what she craved. The comfort and dependability of a normal, mundane life.

But can you return to that normal, mundane life knowing its true cost? The whispers crowded in like a horde of hungry wraiths.

"I've always known the cost of peace," Imani muttered angrily.

You knew it but couldn't comprehend it. Didn't want *to comprehend it. But now you've finally opened your eyes, and you can't unsee it. You can't unknow it. You can't unfeel it.*

"Watch me," she hissed under her breath.

"You win," Niko repeated, snapping her out of her

spiraling thoughts. He stood and pushed away from the table.

Panic rocketed through Imani's chest—he couldn't leave, not before reinforcements arrived. "Wait!"

He froze, then assured, "I'm not going anywhere. I was only going to grab some waters from the fridge. You want one?"

"That's stealing."

He snorted. "I've already murdered millions. Stealing a couple waters from a mega corporation is nothing on my conscience."

"I don't trust you." She motioned for him to sit back down. "I won the game, so you have to do what I want you to, which is stay in place."

Irritation rolled across his expression, but he nonetheless plopped back onto the stool. "I agreed to peacefully go with you to the Marshals. Nothing in the terms stated I couldn't hydrate beforehand. Plus—"

His eyes widened, and then another deeper voice spoke from behind Imani.

"It wasn't a fair game, and you knew it."

"Aiden," Niko sighed.

Imani whirled around and cursed at the sight of another man advancing out from the shadowy depths of the shelves. Her shoulders tensed when she recognized the glint of a gun barrel aimed straight at her. It was an old world gun, the type that used physical projectiles. "That's awful for the environment," she said. "It leaves litter."

"Aiden, put the gun down," Niko said. "Trust me, I have the situation under control."

"I knew it!" Imani's gaze darted between the

former Player and former Referee. Turncoats, both of them. Internally, her brain was freaking out over the weapon aimed at her. Externally, this translated to her mouth blabbering on without control. "This was your backup plan if you lost. Have your traitor friend come rescue you."

Both Iconoclasts ignored her.

"Aiden, put down the gun," Niko repeated.

The former Referee lowered his aim by a couple centimeters. "She's a loose end we can't leave hanging."

"I'm going with her," Niko said. "I made a deal, and I'm going to honor it. Here, take my jacket. It won't do me any good in prison." He shrugged the black coat off and laid it on the table. A crack of bitterness fissured into his voice. "You know, she had a very valid reason for initiating our game. One life for hundreds of thousands? No wonder they think we're the bad guys. Since when did we become the villains, Aiden?"

"You're upset I didn't tell you why the squares were being fogged." Still keeping the gun trained on Imani, Aiden crept close enough to snag the weatherproof jacket and fling it over a shoulder. To Niko, he continued, "I was just trying to protect you from a world of hurt. You knowing would've changed nothing."

"I could've bargained—"

"You would've been arrested on sight, if not killed."

"I had the right to know," Niko snapped.

Aiden flinched, and Imani's nape prickled at the intensity in Niko's utterance.

Niko stood and walked closer, ignoring Aiden's scowl. "You told me the Iconoclasts were seekers of truth." He stopped until he stood between Aiden and

Imani. A barrier of flesh and bone and blood. Only then did Aiden lower the gun with a huff. "You told me willful ignorance is why society is comfortable accepting mass murder as a justifiable means to peace."

Imani gulped and peered around Niko's broad frame, watching the frown deepen on Aiden's face. How did her day get so strange? The man she was trying to turn in was defending her against a fellow Iconoclast.

"I didn't want you to hurt any more than you have already," Aiden said.

Niko's tone softened. "I know. But I'm still leaving with Imani. Once we're gone, return to the Iconoclasts. Everybody wins this way." He cracked a weak chuckle. "Ha, see it *is* possible for both sides to win."

"Oh, hells no." Aiden shook his head and skewered Imani with a glare. "That made-up game was stacked even worse than the Battle Games, so that's really saying something."

Imani retorted before she could help herself. *"Maybe* there are certain aspects of the Battle Games that aren't completely fair, but the world was never a fair place to begin with."

Aiden scoffed. "Gods, listening to you defend your precious Games made my eardrums shrivel up."

She shuddered. How long had he been watching from the shadows? She grabbed onto Niko's arm and took a step toward the exit, using him as a human shield. "Don't even think about shooting."

"What, you're seriously going to march him like that to the nearest enforcement Hub?" Aiden called out.

Niko compliantly let her maneuver him around the table. Unwanted guilt trickled through Imani's veins.

Somehow, she would feel better if he'd resisted. Either that, or if she could somehow shed her sympathy and regain the indifference she'd harbored toward Niko Vandes' fate prior to meeting him. The complicated knot of emotions sitting in her stomach made her want to retch.

"So what if I do?" she challenged. "Are you going to follow us back out into the open? You're a wanted criminal. Exposing yourself is a death—"

The door to the outside corridor whipped opened with a *bang* followed by a sharp voice bellowing, "Marshals! Hands up!"

"Aiden, *no!*" Niko screamed at the same time the green-eyed man spun toward the incoming guards, gun raised and trigger finger primed.

The loud discharges of the old world gun ricocheted off the walls. So unlike the high-pitched whine of the electro-rifles wielded by the newcomers. Imani's ears rang as waves of panic crashed through her body. She battled the urge to release Niko and hide under a table, hands clasped over her ears. Instead, she remain rooted, appalled at the scene unfolding around her.

Aiden never stood a chance, not when he was the sole target of a highly trained Marshal squad. The air electrified, made the hair rise along Imani's arms. Six crackling blue arcs leapt across the space and drove into Aiden's body. His limbs twitched and danced, mouth contorted in a gasping shriek.

The acrid stench of burnt flesh assaulted her nose, and the sting of charged air danced across the roof of her mouth.

The thud of Aiden's body hitting the floor rang louder than the gunshots.

Niko yanked out of Imani's grip, lunging toward Aiden only to be halted by a guard snagging the back of his shirt. A broken cry fell out of Niko's lips as he stared at Aiden.

"Oh shit oh shit oh shit," Imani whispered, pivoting in place to take in the scene. Things were happening at warp speed while her mind was stuck in the mud.

Six fully armored Marshals surrounded her and Niko. One lingered behind, their arm hanging oddly from the socket. (Presumably the one Aiden had wounded.)

"Hands up *now*," the team leader ordered. She primed her rifle and aimed it at Imani while the other guards forced Niko to the ground.

Coppery fear clogged the back of Imani's throat as she raised her arms. Sure, she'd been prepared for this less-than-heroic reception, but on some level, she'd secretly been hoping only Niko would end up in cuffs.

"Holy hells, is that Niko Vandes?" a Marshal with a gruff voice asked.

"Yes," Imani said, careful to keep her hands visible. "I purposely triggered Ulo—uh, the universal lock override to call your attention to his whereabouts."

"Interesting," the leader intoned. "We'll look into your claims later on. For now, you're under arrest for illegal trespassing on personal property." The woman swung her steely stare onto Niko. "Both of you, on your knees and hands behind your heads."

Everything will be okay once the details are cleared up, Imani reassured herself as she complied. Niko mirrored her movements, tears gathering in the corners of his eyes. It was a jarring and disquieting sight that made Imani uncomfortable. This wasn't the beloved Player the world knew, the one who had mastered a stoic Game face and only ever expressed joy and appreciation over his victories. This was a revolutionary who'd barely tasted freedom and love before both were snatched away.

Niko locked eyes with her and deadpanned, "Congratulations on your victory. To the team lead, he said, "Imani tells the truth. I gave her my word I would allow myself to be peacefully taken into custody should she win." He tipped his head toward the abandoned game. "Which she did."

"Is that so?" the guard hovering closest to Niko asked. "Because *peaceful* was the last thing we walked in on."

Somebody else muttered, "First Vandes going rogue and now being outplayed by some random citizen? The world must be ending."

A burly man approached Niko while a stout woman marched up to Imani. Niko's face twisted into a grimace as the man viciously yanked his arms back and slapped on cuffs. The female Marshal was gentler with Imani, putting on the cuffs just tight enough so they wouldn't slip off. The barrel-chested guard manhandling Niko hauled him up, a venomous cruelness in his movements.

"You'll pay for this, Vandes," he growled. "My sister was living in one of the squares fogged two days ago. She died because of your cowardice."

Niko opened his mouth to respond but the guard slammed the butt of his rifle into Vandes' temple, and the former Player dropped like a pigeon struck by lightning.

Imani hid a wince. She didn't want the guards thinking she harbored sympathetic sentiments for a traitor. Because she didn't. Niko deserved every last ounce of agony headed his way. At least that's what Imani told herself.

The team lead pivoted and marched for the door. Her words were a snapped order. "Get them loaded into truck twenty-nine."

Two guards dragged Vandes' unconscious body like he was already a dead man. A third guard hoisted Aiden over a shoulder and followed.

They ascended to the first floor, then out the main entrance and back outside. Imani squinted in the sudden brightness cast by the blue and red sirens. Three armored vehicles were parked outside of the building, lights strobing against the sunset. Another half dozen Marshals guarded the area.

"Imani!" Kit's voice sliced through the chaos pummeling inside her skull.

She twisted and spotted them waving their arm. Then their jaw dropped as their gaze slid behind her. She glanced over her shoulder. Closed her eyes at the sight of Aiden's lifeless limbs. Already, a Marshal was striding over with a biodegradable body bag in hand.

He would be alive if it weren't for me. She hadn't meant to kill him. She *didn't* kill him, not really. It was the Marshals who did that. So why did the weight of Aiden's death press against her chest like an iron block? Why did she even care about the life of a traitor, of a stranger?

She'd succeeded in stopping Niko Vandes from causing more harm. She should be happy! But her fingers and shoulders wouldn't stop shaking, whether from stress or despair, she couldn't say.

"Oh, Imani," Kit's voice carried on the ocean-tinged breeze, sad and disappointed. "What have you done?"

She didn't want to know.

CHAPTER 12
NIKO

NIKO FLOATED IN THE SPACE BETWEEN thoughts, suspended in that liminal dimension between consciousness and not. An unsettling hyper awareness of his own mind filtered through his neurons. Each thought bellowed as loud as an avalanche yet lumbered slow as a glacier.

Oh, and he was cold.

So, so cold he was burning.

"Niko, can you hear me?"

The voices came from above, a choir beckoning. Was this heaven?

"Niko?"

No, that wasn't possible. Only eternal damnation awaited him after death. Which meant this must be a dream . . .

"He should be awake."

"Niko, listen to me. Follow my voice."

Peeling his eyes open was a momentous task requiring all his strength. Ice-fire burned through his veins. He blinked. Blinked again. When his vision refused to focus, panic clawed up his throat as he struggled to sit except his muscles refused to listen and he couldn't feel anything aside from the blistering cold invading his body and—

"Whoa, his heart rate's spiking—"

"Niko. You're okay."

He grasped onto that distant voice then croaked, "Can't see."

Had he gone blind? No, not fully blind. Colors bled across his vision like paint dripping down a wall. Blurry silhouettes hovered nearby, ink blots on a watercolor background. The ink blots resembled monsters and demons and—

"Do you know where you are, Niko?"

"Hell?" he asked hopefully, because the alternative would be worse.

A chuckle sounded to his right. "Glad you still have your sense of humor."

"Niko Vandes." A deeper voice, a different speaker. "You have been arrested for treason against international peace, violation against the Battle Game Accords, and thirty-seven other lesser offenses. Currently, you are under custody of the International Conflict Resolution Court."

"I feel weird."

"It's the Veratim," the person who'd laughed earlier explained. "You might feel a bit disconnected, but that's normal. I'm Dr. Khala. My job is to make sure we have the right dosage so you're feeling nice and relaxed, but not too much we lose you completely."

"You mean, make me go insane?" Niko tried to raise his head, and failed.

His mind floated in its own sphere, disjointed from the rest of his physical self. Sure, he was aware of the aches and pains radiating from his right arm and ribs, but his brain registered the sensation with the detached coolness of a cat watching a fly walk across a windowpane. Or maybe the *others* were the cat and he was the fly they were observing. He wondered if there was a one-way window into whatever gods-forsaken room he was trapped in. If there was a team of interrogators and analysts ready to pick him apart, both figuratively and literally. And gods, he was so cold, maybe he could ask someone to turn up the—

"Focus on my voice." Dr. Khala yanked Niko's attention back like a dog on a chain. "I know Veratim takes some getting used to, but try to work with me, okay?"

Veratim. He'd heard of it before. A tailored hallucinogenic that made it difficult to think straight, made the mind susceptible to outside influences. *A tool for humane interrogation,* Peaceful Ends had pitched it. *Veratim minimizes suffering while maximizing success.*

"Okay," Niko said.

"Marshal Hall and I are going to ask a few questions. Focus on answering them, all right? Ignore everything else and only think about those questions."

"Okay," he repeated, hating how laborious it was just to wrangle that one word off his tongue.

Normally, his mind raced at warp speed, thoughts processing through dozens of strands simultaneously. Now, he could barely hold onto a single thought at a time. If his mind was his sharpest weapon, then the drug had blunted him.

"How did you meet Aiden Tays?" Marshal Hall, the deeper voice, asked.

A spike of pain sheared through Niko's chest. "Is he okay?"

"Answer the question."

Maybe Aiden had survived the electric shock. He'd seen Aiden fall, but that didn't mean he was *dead*. Perhaps the medics revived Aiden. Hope shot through his veins—

"Niko, focus," Dr. Khala's oil-smooth voice interjected. "How did you meet Aiden Tays?"

How could they expect him to *focus* when he didn't know if Aiden was dead or alive or being tortured—

"Aiden Tays is dead," Marshal Hall stated. "How did you meet him?"

"No . . ." Niko didn't know if he was protesting Aiden's death or refusing to answer their questions. Didn't care anymore. The last flicker of hope extinguished, plunging the inside of his mind into crushing darkness.

Aiden and millions of others, dead. Surely he belonged with the deceased. Why did he deserve to live while others perished? Was he just *lucky,* that chance always played in his favor? Maybe this was all for vain. He'd sacrificed his family and Aiden and countless others for hope of a better future—and that was the crux of it all, the *hope.* An intangible, fragile thing that promised everything but guaranteed nothing.

The Marshal grunted. "Increase the dosage."

"We're already near the limit," Dr. Khala replied. Their conversation floated above Niko, who was too trapped inside his own mind to care about his fate. "Any more and he'll start experiencing severe disassociation and risk of permanent damage."

"Do it. If I had it my way, Vandes would've been euthanized already. But the Court doesn't want to accidentally martyr him by killing him off too soon." Marshal Hall leaned down, so close to Niko's face he could make out distinctive features despite his compromised vision. Sunken eyes. A slightly crooked nose. Thick brows and a strong jaw. "Do it now, Doctor."

The Marshal smiled, bright white teeth elongating into fangs as a fresh rush of Veratim surged through Niko's blood. It was poison burrowing into his flesh like maggots.

And his mind was collapsing in on itself, a star that had gone supernova then imploded into a blackhole.

WHEN HIS MIND FINALLY CLEARED HOURS?—days?—weeks?—later, Niko wished he still had the drug numbing his thoughts. Anything to dull the piercing agony that splintered his insides every time he remembered *Aiden was dead*. Nope. He couldn't deal with confronting that thought yet.

So he let it fester untouched. Aiden's death sat lodged between his ribs like a piece of shrapnel. He let the hurt linger—removing it meant bleeding out. Gods, if Aiden's death hurt this much, how much pain must Ivonna be in? While he'd been focused on his Iconoclast mission, it'd been easy to shove thoughts of Ivonna to the wayside. But now with nothing but time at his disposal, grief pushed through the cracks in his thoughts. Grief for a family he wished he could've known better before it was too late. Grief for Ivonna, who'd lost her daughter, parents, and siblings. Grief for the bond broken between Coach and Player, mother and son.

Niko's chest ached so fiercely he feared a heart attack, so he directed his attention onto his physical hurt instead. He licked his chapped lips then patted his arms, chest, and legs. Everything felt bruised but otherwise intact. He still couldn't see, not even blurs of colors or silhouettes. Everything was pitch dark. In a shock of panic, his fingers flew up and probed at his eye sockets, confirming his eyeballs hadn't been popped like lychees squeezed out of their shells.

Both eyeballs, check. Either he was being kept in a sensory deprivation cell, or he'd been permanently blinded.

"I warned you wouldn't like the alternative if you didn't cooperate." Marshal Hall's voice surrounded him like the guilt plaguing Niko. "I tried to be nice. Humane. You didn't appreciate the mercy of not feeling, so now you'll have to feel *everything*."

"I don't remember much of what happened before," Niko spoke to the darkness. "But if you weren't getting the answers you wanted about the Iconoclasts, it's because I truly don't know anything."

"*Anything?*" Hall's insidious chuckle winded through the air. The room's sound system was top tier. "That smells like a lie."

Niko shrugged, wincing when the motion tugged on his sides. "I'd barely joined the Iconoclasts for a week. You think they're dumb enough to tell newcomers their secrets?"

"But you *do* know a lot about Aiden Tays."

Silence seeped into the room. Niko's heart thundered in his ears.

"Truth be told, I wished my colleagues had shot you instead." Hall's voice sounded from behind Niko this time.

Me too, he thought bitterly.

Hall's voice rang from the right. "Tays is an enigma. A vault of information waiting to be cracked. If I weren't so disgusted by his involvement with terrorism—"

"You mean trying to stop systematic murdering?" Niko snarled.

"I would've been impressed with how cleverly he had us all fooled. Alas, we don't have Tays. We have you, the next best thing. And you will give us *everything* you have on Tays. His quirks and habits, his favorite restaurants and hobbies, his weaknesses and strengths."

Without Veratim slowing his thoughts, Niko instantly saw the Marshal's goal. By reconstructing Aiden's life, the Marshal hoped to use it as a starting point for tracking down other Iconoclast leads.

His jaw tightened. He wouldn't betray Aiden or the Iconoclasts. He'd sworn an oath when he joined, and he wouldn't break it. Not even if it meant breaking his own bones and spilling his own blood and losing his own mind.

The revolution must live on. Words Aiden had whispered to Niko in the cabin in the mountains, reveling in each other's company. *Protect the revolution at all costs.*

Niko had traced his gaze over Aiden's refined brows and nose. *Sounds romantic. Is the revolution to be my one true love?*

Aiden's mouth had twisted into something savage. *I warned you not to romance a revolution. But if you're so determined to, understand she's an insatiable lover. She'll take and take and take, and you won't get anything in return except the knowledge you're securing a better future.* A mischievous twinkle appeared in his eyes. *Or you can take my advice and make* me *your one true love. The revolution is a reason to fight for. I'm your reason to live for.*

Niko's love for Aiden was complicated, much like his love for Ivonna. But at the end of the day, love was still love, no matter how deeply that love might cut. Niko had failed to protect Ivonna. He couldn't let Aiden's memory be tarnished.

"You know, I thought you were supposed to be smart," Hall said. "But only a fool would join the Iconoclasts when they already had everything they could desire."

Everything but freedom of choice. Aiden had promised freedom. Niko wasn't sure if he'd delivered. Nonetheless, Niko tilted his head and flashed an insolent grin. "I suppose I am a fool."

A thin beam of light appeared, outlining the door as it slid open. He rose to his feet and lifted his chin, eyes squinting against the sudden brightness.

Marshal Hall appeared in the entryway, the backlight washing out any discernible features. "In the past, fools were court entertainers." He strode forward, letting more light fill the small room. A knife lazily spun in his palm. His deep blue eyes locked onto Niko's as he crooned, "Sing for me, fool."

CHAPTER 13

IMANI

THE PRESIDENT'S COMMENDATION MEDAL, the highest honor a citizen could receive, sat heavy as a grenade in Imani's hand when she stepped out of the court house and into the waiting claws of the press.

"Over here, Ms. Tenzing!"

"Do you plan on retiring with your award money?"

"Is it true all charges were dropped against you?"

"Imani!" An intrepid reporter broke past the security barricade providing a clear passage to her waiting vehicle. "Daton, Global Reporter. How's it feel to be the hero who saved international peace?"

Twenty cameras zoomed in on her. She wished it was Ulo clenched in her hand and not the unfamiliar medal. Her thumb brushed over the metallic surface, seeking buttons that didn't exist. "I . . . I feel overwhelmed."

Daton nodded empathetically. "Very understandable—the whole world was dismayed to discover Niko Vandes wasn't the star Player he pretended to be, but a terrorist all along. It makes one wonder if any of us actually knew the true Niko in the first place. Well, since you encountered Vandes in the flesh, what *was* he like when he's off the screen and away from the board?"

"Calm," was the first word that popped into Imani's head. Niko had been unexpectedly easy going, all things considered.

"Calm?" Daton raised a brow then shook away Imani's response with a laugh. "Did Vandes try to attack you? Is it true he shot his partner while trying to escape the Marshals?"

She stiffened, hiding her revulsion at Daton's delight in his speculating. "Niko actually tried to protect me from being shot."

The reporter stared at her blankly, like he wasn't computing her words. "I'm sorry, are we talking about the same Niko Vandes here? The one who cheated the Game and—"

Daton's voice droned into the background as Imani hunched her shoulders and marched toward the waiting car. Her stomach knotted itself into a nauseous lump. Every description the reporter had associated with Niko fit her preconceptions of the Player prior to meeting him. Hells, *she'd* been surprised Niko hadn't resorted to violence and bloodshed, when she'd been ready to take a swing at him. But the reality of Niko proved he wasn't what she'd thought him to be—either as a Player or as an Iconoclast. Her steps slowed as the revelation of such implications forced her to reconsider what she *thought* she knew about the Iconoclasts. About the Games. About . . . everything she thought she understood.

It'd been easy to pin the Iconoclasts as the villains. How dare they criticize the Battle Games that'd saved humanity from destroying itself? The Games were so integrated into the very fabric of the world it was akin to criticizing the sun for shining. But just because something was familiar didn't make it right. It was too easy to confuse familiarity for something good.

Imani reached the car and raised her gaze in time to catch a figure standing at the edge of the crowd. Her heart lifted, and she wondered if they'd also attended the award ceremony earlier. "Kit!"

She turned to the driver holding open the door, intent on letting him know Kit would be riding with them, but when she looked back up, Kit had vanished and she felt more alone than ever.

In all her years working as a custodian, Imani had never taken more than three days off consecutively. So her two-week-long vacation had her spinning in place, at a loss of where to go. (Figuratively, of course. She'd been delighted to return back to the comforts of her own home and was quite content to remain there for the duration of her time off.)

The initial crush of reporters banging on her door had finally trickled down as the news set their crosshairs on Niko's imprisonment instead. Imani's gut roiled at the thought of Niko's impending trial—no doubt he would be found guilty and euthanized.

And it was all her fault.

She didn't regret turning in Niko, not if the alternative meant more squares being fogged. But she *was* mad—at the International Conflict Resolution Court for punishing the very same citizens they were supposed to protect, simply because of a Player gone rogue. A government that harmed its own people to *make a point* had no business being a government.

Pacing the length of her kitchen, Imani stared at the *No new messages* display on her tablet. Despair threatened to choke her out. She couldn't let Niko die, not when she finally understood why he so badly wanted to take down the Battle Games. And, incredibly, Imani actually believed he might have a shot of making real change *if* she could free him. But despite pulling on all her strings and favors in hopes of finding contact with the Iconoclasts, she'd been left screaming into the void with nary an echo. (Seriously, not even a bounced message.)

Which left Kit. She was 99.83% confident they were an Iconoclast and her best chance of saving Niko. Except she had no way of contacting them—the last time Imani saw Kit had been outside of the courthouse, and the last time she'd heard from them was when they'd furiously messaged, *Stop mentioning my name to the reporters, I don't want any association with the Vandes debacle.* Aside from that, they'd either blocked or was ignoring her calls and texts. She didn't even know where they lived. But she *did* know where they worked . . .

Her fingers twitched, nerves worn ragged from the countless dead ends and departure from the routine schedule she'd grown dependent on. Yes, perhaps returning to work was a good idea. Plus, no way Kit could ignore her when she was physically in front of their face, right?

*

IMANI GLOWERED AT HER CURRY AND RICE, SHOV-eling another spoonful and gnashing her teeth. Everything tasted like bone chips and ash.

"Why are you glaring at your lunch like it personally offended you?" Oran asked from across the picnic table where the Custodian team was taking their midday break outside. He snuck his spoon into Imani's container to steal a bite. "Mmmmm, delicious. It's illegal to be in a sour mood when eating good food."

She snorted. "It's not *good,* it's good enough."

Kit cocked their head, overhearing her mumbled comment. Their eyes narrowed, but they didn't say anything. As it turned out, Kit *could* ignore Imani even when she was right in front of their face. At least it was a professional cold shoulder—they still cooperated with Imani when on the job. But Kit never initiated talk or joked anymore, and that hurt more than she cared to admit.

"Seriously, Kit, you've got to try it." Oran scooped another spoonful of curry. "This is the best thing since sliced bagels."

"Bread," they corrected and took a prim bite of their chicken-and-tomato sandwich. (How anyone could happily eat two dry pieces of untoasted bread with a slab of grilled chicken and slice of tomato with the gusto Kit imbued was beyond Imani.) "Thanks, but no thanks. I've got to start working on the repair items."

They popped the last bit of sandwich into their mouth and rose from the table, snagging a toolbox from the floor as they meandered over to the garage.

Today was maintenance day, which meant the team

would be performing the monthly vehicle upkeeps, software updates, and haz suit checkouts. As it were, several of the garage bay doors were opened, allowing glimpses into the building's cavernous interior.

Imani stared at Kit's retreating form for a few seconds then stood. If they wanted to play hard-to-catch, *fine.* She sped after Kit, who had vanished into the garage where the vans and drones were kept. Custodians from a different team worked on their own vehicle dozens of meters away. The other team's laughter and cheerful voices echoed in the large, open room. Longing twisted at Imani's heart—she missed the camaraderie she used to share with Kit.

She spotted them at the rear wall, beside the workbench running its length.

Their shoulders stiffened at her approach but they didn't look up from the drone they were tinkering with.

She moved closer and swung her voice down to a whisper. "I need your help."

They flicked her a snide side eye. "What for? You have fame and wealth and everything you could ever want."

"I know who you are. *What* you are."

They unscrewed a propeller from the drone and placed it on the balancer, frowning when the blades listed to the side. Tossing the damaged rotor into the recycle bin, they grabbed a new set from the spares container and ensured it was properly balanced before bolting it onto the drone. "Oh yeah? Tell me, then."

"Let's talk in the community garden."

They set down the mag driver and moved onto checking the drone's battery health. "Trying to get me isolated . . . Should I be concerned? Am I going to wind up a missing person? Murdered and fed to the trees?"

Imani grabbed the battery diagnostics gadget from the toolbox and handed it over. "I'm not trying to threaten or blackmail you."

They plugged the diagnostic tool into the power pack. The device beeped green, the battery at 96% health.

When they still didn't respond, she pressed, "I didn't intend for Aiden to get killed and neither do I want Niko to perish. For a long time, I believed keeping my head down and doing my job and being a model citizen was good enough. And maybe for some people—for most people—good enough is, well, good enough."

"But not for you?" Hope glimmered across Kit's eyes before a sharp wariness glazed over, like they were suspicious of Imani's change in tune.

She couldn't blame them. She was responsible for the loss of two Iconoclast agents after all.

"No," she confirmed. "I don't want just *good enough.* I want to do something *good,* something worth doing. Good enough doesn't necessarily mean *good.*"

They flicked a propeller, and Imani tracked the blades spinning smoothly and silently. Satisfied, Kit tucked the drone under an arm and grabbed the pilot's tablet. "You're right, we should talk outside. I need to take this out for a test flight anyway."

Relief loosened the tension that'd been slowly suffocating Imani all week. Kit was willing to listen. Hopefully, they were willing to help too.

Kit broke into a jog, and Imani followed them back outside and down a solar cell walkway to an open meadow planted with native grass. Tiny bee drones the size of her thumb nail buzzed near clusters of wildflowers, keeping the ecosystem pollinated. Like their biological counterparts, the bee drones would only live for a month before they started breaking down, their biodegradable components reclaimed by the earth as nutrients.

"What's with your change in attitude?" Kit asked as they powered on the Custodian drone. With a graceful toss, Kit launched the vehicle into the air and sent it through a series of complex maneuvers, testing out the response of its new blades. "You were perfectly content ignoring all the ugly truths in order to preserve the beautiful lie you wanted to live in."

"Meeting Niko, talking with you, having a whole week to myself with nothing to do but reflect on what I know. Such as the fact you're an"—her voice pulled back, as if uttering the name too loud would summon the Marshals—"*Iconoclast.*"

"What makes you think I'm one?"

"For one, you're not denying my statement as any sane person immediately would. Second, Niko said the *exact* same thing you told me earlier: complacency is the death of progress. Doesn't take a genius to realize that's one of *their* mottos."

"That's actually my quote," Kit deadpanned. "The organization borrowed it."

Imani gaped. "You're kidding, right? Are you, like, high up in the hierarchy?"

"I'm as serious as a cow playing a piano."

"But that's not very serious?"

"Rightfully noted." They raised her an imaginary hat, still maintaining a straight face. But that familiar warm twinkle was back, promising of mischief and understanding. A sign Imani was slowly working her way back into their good graces.

"Well, if complacency is the death of progress, then ennui is the death of the human spirit. Humans are meant to *feel*. To live without passion is to simply exist, not live. Back when I was complacent with pretending the consequences of the Battle Games didn't exist and not caring about other people's hardships so long as it didn't affect *me?* That was . . . I wasn't really living. I was just existing in a bubble I felt comfortable in. I don't want that anymore. I want *reality* with all its filth and hate and love and despair and hope."

Kit stretched out a palm and the drone landed on it like a hummingbird. The buzz of its rotors cut off, leaving the *shh-shh* of the tall grass to fill the silence. For the first time in weeks, they looked her in the eye, and held it. "Sounds like the only reason why you changed is for purely selfish reasons."

She opened her mouth to protest but they waved her off, continuing in a matter-of-fact tone.

"*You* didn't want to live a passionless life. *You* didn't want to ignore reality. *You* didn't want to settle for good enough." A pause. "Am I wrong?"

Imani bit her lower lip, curbing the instinct to defend herself. Instead, she took a deep breath and nodded. "Fine. Call me a selfish bastard. At least I'm a selfish, *honest* bastard who's trying to do the right thing. It's better to do the right things for the wrong reasons than vice versa, no?"

A contemplative grin crept across Kit's face. "An interesting philosophical question. I reckon it depends on what matters more: intention or outcome. Does the thought matter—"

"Look, I need your help," Imani interjected before Kit could sidetrack them with a debate. "I've tried reaching out to others for help but nobody's willing."

"Define *others*."

Her mouth twisted as she admitted, "The Iconoclasts. Nobody responded."

"Gee, I wonder why. What makes you think *I'll* be willing to help?"

She braced her shoulders and decided to put it all out there. Either Kit trusted her, or they didn't. She'd initially resisted the idea of dragging them deeper into her mess, but she was out of options. "I want to rescue Niko Vandes."

Kit's fingers squeezed the drone and snapped its rotor in half. They stared down at the broken pieces. "Dammit, I literally *just* fixed it."

"Will you help me?"

"How do I know you're not laying down a trap?"

"Here, take this." She took out the memory chip Niko had given her. "It's from Vandes. Supposedly it contains information your lot wanted."

Quick as a scorpion, Kit snatched the tiny metal square and examined it before tucking it away. "Looks like one of the encrypted memory chips the organization uses. But then again, maybe you've uploaded malware onto it to spy on our systems."

Shaking her head, she groaned, "Kit Hart, you are one paranoid motherfucker."

"It keeps me alive."

"What must I do to convince you I'm on your side?"

"I suppose there might be *one* thing you could do. Putting Niko behind bars really messed up the organization's plans."

She nodded. Of course Niko would play a key role in whatever grand scheme the Iconoclasts had in the works. One simply didn't induct a highly publicized figure without using their fame to its full potential. "What do I need to do?"

"Something dangerous."

"Fine by me."

"Also, I'll have to get permission from the higher-ups first." They turned on their heel and started marching back to the garage bays. "That might take some convincing—or maybe not, because you're the one who'll be carrying all the risks."

"Again, I'm okay with that. Just tell me what I need to do."

They tossed a glance back at Imani and airily replied, "Be Niko Vandes."

CHAPTER 14
NIKO

"YOU HAVE A VISITOR, VANDES." MARSHAL Hall's voice blared through the intercom.

Niko despised the voice. Hated how it scraped across his eardrums and set his teeth on edge. The excruciating white lights flooding the featureless room didn't help either. The sheer brightness of everything—white walls, white floor, white ceiling—burned his retinas and frayed his nerves until the smallest disturbance made him flinch.

"Who, you?" Niko muttered.

His skull pounded so hard his jaw ached, and his right hand throbbed—the cauterized stumps of his ring and pinky fingers a reminder of what'd happened yesterday with Marshal Hall. The sharp, hot pain of the surgical blade slicing through tendons and nerves lingered like unwanted company. Too bad the rest of Niko's memory was a moth hole riddled mess. He couldn't even remember how he'd gone from the pitch-black cell to this blinding-white one. Or maybe it was the same room and they'd simply turned on the lights.

"You wish," Hall scoffed. "Don't worry, we'll tag up afterward. I hope you feel special. Normally visitors aren't allowed."

"I feel *so* special," Niko replied drolly.

He rolled his neck. His head weighed heavy, his mouth thick with cotton. Who would've guessed the International Conflict Resolution Court Corrections Facility was capable of such base violence? For an organization that touted the Battle Games as the more humane method of conflict resolution, cutting off fingers seemed hypocritical. He stared at his mutilated hand and wondered if he'd lost more than just fingers. His sanity, for one. For fuck's sake, he was practically *joking* with the Marshal tasked with breaking him.

Hall snickered. "Visit is five minutes long, starting now."

The door whooshed open and a person stepped through. Niko squinted then stumbled a step back. Pressed a fist into an eye, which only induced a fresh spurt of pain from the bruise and swelling. Nothing made sense. He was hallucinating, he had to be.

"Hello, Niko," the woman said.

To anyone else, she would've sounded distant and unaffected.

To Niko, he barely recognized the thread of emotion winding through those two words. But it was there, as unexpected and foreign as ice in a desert. He stepped forward and continued staring, unblinking for fear she would vanish if he did. "Mother?"

Ivonna's face crumpled for a millisecond before a sterile mien replaced it. No doubt they were being observed and if there was one thing both Niko and

Ivonna were well versed in, it was donning *the mask.*

"Why are you here?" he asked. Guilt flooded in when he realized she looked wrecked. Her slender frame had become borderline skeletal and dark half-moons hung under her eyes. She'd lost her—*their*—family because of him. "I didn't mean to—I never wanted to harm . . ." He swallowed the lump clogging the back of his throat, watching her mask erode into raw grief, and croaked, "I'm so, so sorry."

She must hate him. That was why she was here, right? She'd come to curse and blame him for everything. And he couldn't fault her for that.

"Please forgive me. If there's anything I could've done to prevent it, I would've." He bowed his head, shame crawling down the back of his neck, and braced to receive her tirade.

Sure, some part of him resented Ivonna for forcing his childhood onto a predetermined path—the same path that drove him toward a cliff's edge. But she'd also protected him in her own, misguided way. He didn't want her hurt.

He startled when she grasped him by both shoulders, urging him to meet her eyes. "I'm sad, of course, and angry." A tremor rippled through the indomitable Ivonna's voice. She'd hurt in the aftermath. Hurt more than she would ever admit. "But I'm more relieved you're still alive.

The breath caught in his lungs, unprepared for the tenderness softening her normally steel-hard gaze.

"I'm okay." She continued, voice turning steady and dependable. "You, on the other hand . . ."

He curled his mangled fingers, wincing at the bright

pain. "It could be worse."

She sighed and took a step back, arms wilting down to her sides. "To answer your earlier question, I'm here trying to ensure my son survives." She pinched the bridge of her nose in a rare moment of exhaustion. "Cooperate, Niko. Give them the information they want about the Iconoclasts."

"I honestly don't know—"

"Tell them everything they want to know about Aiden Tays."

He recoiled. "Absolutely not."

"Aiden's dead. There's no point protecting him. *You're* alive. Focus on protecting yourself."

He shook his head and half turned away from her. She didn't understand he wasn't trying to protect Aiden, but rather the memory of him—of them. Of the revolution.

Protect the revolution at all costs.

"The Iconoclasts stand no chance. Be smart and jump ship before it sinks," Ivonna urged. "Cooperate, Niko, then you can come home. I've already worked out the terms with the Court."

He choked out a soft laugh. "Home? Where's that? Back to the academy grounds, so I can continue being a pawn? Oh, wait—I've been banned from the Games for life."

She blew a hard breath through her nose, a tiny frown creasing her forehead. "What's your plan then? Your end game? Are you going to languish here, in pain and in vain, waiting for a rescue from the organization that has abandoned you?" Her eyes narrowed, feline and just a touch feral. A vestige of the savage Player she once was. "I didn't teach you to play a losing game. If your current strategy isn't working, then *pivot.* Try a different tactic. Don't wait around and hope victory will find its way to you."

"You taught me not to surrender. Taught me not to give what my opponents want."

"I'm not telling you to concede defeat," she reprimanded. "I'm telling you to change your game plan instead of playing straight into your demise."

"Giving in to the Marshals *will* ki—"

"What's the First Rule?"

"Control the board," he recited.

Her eyes flashed as she pinned him with a pointed stare.

Oh. *Oh.*

Of course Niko had considered the possibility the Iconoclasts would cut their losses when he got caught. But he'd needed hope to preserve the scraps of sanity left, and so he'd clung onto the chance that they would swoop in with a rescue. He'd ceded control of his fate to the Iconoclasts.

Chance or control. No, he wouldn't fall into the trap of waiting for a chance to escape—he was going to take control of the situation and *make* his escape happen.

Ivonna must've caught the moment her cryptic message clicked because she gave a satisfied nod. "Don't forget your roots."

"I won't."

She glanced at the utility-band wrapped around her wrist. "I've got one minute left before they kick me out." A couple seconds passed in silence, then she whispered, "Why?"

A single word carrying a hundred different questions.

"Because peace is something worth fighting for."

She raised a dark brow and opened her mouth, ready to voice her own opinion but Niko cut her off. "War will find peace and corrupt it if the reason behind the war is not addressed. But never has peace stumbled into war and soothed its thorns—peace needs to be actively sought, worked toward, *fought* for. The Battle Games were supposed to be the eco-friendly equalizer, and maybe they were, at first. But we can do better than that. There *must* be a way to resolve conflicts without resorting to mass murder. Why not treat all the countries the way the Archipelago provinces are represented in the national ruling house? If two nations can't come to an agreement, then have other countries cast their votes on the final outcome."

He waved a hand at Ivonna's unconvinced expression. "The point is, there are other ways out there worth exploring."

"You remind me of my younger self, sometimes," she murmured, then scowled at the ceiling when Marshal Hall blared through the hidden speakers.

"Ivonna Vandes, please exit the room."

He clenched his jaw at Hall's intruding voice. Ivonna carefully wiped away her displeasure, a neutral mask sliding down her expression. Niko almost grabbed onto her arm as she stepped away, questions hanging off the tip of his tongue. *Do you want a way out of your life? Do you want to join the Iconoclasts?*

But he couldn't make offers he couldn't follow through with, so he simply watched her straighten her shoulders and march toward the egress.

*

Niko had a game plan. A battle plan.

A plan that was quickly falling apart as he crept along a corridor flashing with orange emergency lights. His muffled breaths were the only sounds, the silence eerie in the murkiness. No alarms blared, no shouts echoed down the hall. The only indication his escape had been noticed was the ominous flashing lights. Perhaps adrenaline was making him lightheaded, because his head spun and vertigo threatened his balance every other step.

It'd been laughingly easy to escape the cell once Niko put his mind to it. He'd played the role of a defeated prisoner willing to talk, and Hall lapped up every tidbit of information Niko spilled about Aiden.

I'm sorry, Niko apologized to his ghost. *But the revolution must live on.*

Afterward, Niko had stolen the key from Hall—nimble fingers, thanks to Aiden's many cardistry lessons. A pang had stabbed through Niko's gut at the reminder of Aiden. He'd swallowed away the bitter, guilt-tinged grief, still not ready to confront it.

No one was more surprised than Niko that his plan had unrolled without a hitch. It'd been easy to stroll out. Suspiciously easy. When the orange lights triggered ten seconds later, Niko knew he'd been *allowed* to leave the cell. He suspected this was all a game to Marshal Hall.

A game he didn't know the rules to.

Exhaustion pulled on his limbs, hunger and thirst twisting his insides. He had to get out of here, but he was a rat in a maze. No windows or signages indicated whether he should go up or down to find the exit.

Upward it is. If he found himself on the roof and backed into a corner, at least he would still have an escape off this cursed building. Even if the escape promised a certain death. Plus, he'd rather his last view be of the starry night and not artificial lights and impersonal walls.

Niko's thighs burned as he climbed another flight of stairs. Sweat beaded along his forehead. Damn, he was more out of shape than he realized. A door welcomed him at the top of the landing and swung open beneath his touch. A click snicked the air when it closed after him. He gave a tentative twist of the handle—locked.

Well. No way forward but up. He scanned the corners of the stairwell, wondering if hidden cameras monitored his every move, then ascended yet another flight of stairs. A cool breeze blew through the opened set of doors on the next landing. Waiting for him.

Fuck. This was definitely a trap.

What sort of mind game was Hall playing at? Was it even *legal?*

I'm a Court Marshal. Hall's earlier words spun through Niko's brain. *My word is as good as the law, my actions the will of the Court.*

Dread piling inside his rib cage, Niko slipped through the opened doors and onto the rooftop. A two meter high fence surrounded the perimeter. He walked to the edge and peered down the sides of the building. Solar pavement greeted him at least twenty stories below. Low lumen pole lights offered illumination in ten meter intervals along the fence. The moon hung in the sky, and when he closed his eyes and focused, the gentle lullaby of the ocean sang in the distance. Without the menacing orange lights, it was almost serene.

He followed the rooftop perimeter, slowing his pace to catch his breath while also searching for a gap in the electrified fencing and a potential path down the outside face of the building. His thin-slippered feet came to a halt when a familiar silhouette appeared on the horizon.

Paxania Stadium.

The arena's distinctive crown-shaped geometry was unmistakable, each point of its jagged spires lit with a gem-like light. The roar of the crowd echoed in Niko's ears, followed by the sickening thrill of being declared victor of Game after Game after Game.

"Quite a sight, isn't it?"

Niko startled and spun toward the voice that haunted his nightmares. Anxiety crackled down his spine and sweat surfaced in his palms.

Marshal Hall melted out of the shadows and meandered over. He followed Niko's line of sight to the stadium. "The 30th annual Peacetime Games will commence in two days."

A chasm opened in Niko's stomach. "Two days? But the Peacetime Games aren't until—"

"The end of summer?" Hall crossed his arms and sent Niko a sideways glance. A dozen guards seeped out from the darkness, silent as wraiths, surrounding them. "You've been here for forty-five days."

Niko staggered, nearly pitching into the electrified fencing. Hall's hand shot out and snatched the front of his shirt, hauling him away from the edge.

"That's why I feel so weak," Niko murmured to himself. He hadn't imagined losing so much weight and stamina.

Hall nodded. "Stasis longer than a week tends to be hard on the body."

Niko flicked his gaze out to Paxania Stadium then back to the Marshal. "Am I to participate in the upcoming Games?"

Hall released Niko's shirt but didn't step away nor stop the guards from tightening their semi-circle. "Yes, you'll be in the Peacetime Games."

"But not as a Player."

Hall offered a wolfish grin, which Niko translated as a *yes*.

Niko stepped up to the fence, ignoring the Marshal tensing in his periphery. "Not a Player, but a martyr."

"A traitor," Hall corrected. "A criminal. A pawn for the filthy rebels, an example to be made."

The buzz of electricity coursing through the barbed wires hummed in the air. Niko wondered how many amps raced through the metal strands—enough to knock him out? Stop his heart permanently? "You promised I could go home if I cooperated."

What would hurt more if he grabbed onto the fence: the wicked barbs, or the electric shock?

"Why else do you think you're returning to Paxania Stadium? It's where you belong."

Niko raised an arm, flexing the remaining three fingers on his right hand.

Hall cleared his throat. "Vandes, I advise you step back from the edge. Don't make me regret releasing you from stasis early."

"Oh yeah?" The hair along Niko's arm prickled, from anticipation and potential charging through the wires. "Why *did* you wake me, then? Why let me waltz out and come up here?"

"Because I'm not merciless. Do you know how many strings I had to pull to orchestrate this? I wanted to gift you one last thrill—"

"Before I'm put down in front of thousands of people." Niko glared at Hall and gestured between them, then at the guards. "If this your idea of a *game,* you're real messed up."

Hall frowned, shadows passing his features like a dark fog. "Don't lie, Vandes. I know you must've felt an adrenaline rush when you slipped out of the cell. A real-life game of Labyrinth. As a Marshal, I'm not supposed to have favorites, but you were always mine. I've watched every one of your matches, seen each post victory interview. I still remember, after your tenth Battle Game win, a reporter asked *What's your favorite part of playing?* You replied, *The thrill of closing a Game.*"

Niko rolled his eyes. "If you're waiting for me to thank you, please, hold your breath. Then maybe you'll asphyxiate and die."

"Get away from the fence *now,*" Hall ordered.

Niko grinned and raised his gaze to the night sky. He wanted his last view to be of the constellations wheeling overhead. Some part of him despised his intentions, accused him of giving up. But hadn't he tried enough? And he was so, so tired.

A small object darted across the sky. He paused, eyes squinting. A red light flashed a couple times then went dark. A drone. Nobody else seemed to have noticed, all their attention laser focused on him.

The tiny vehicle dipped, hovering half a dozen meters above Niko, close enough he recognized it as a Custodian drone. Strange. As an internationally recognized neutral territory, Paxania Island had never experienced Karlo's ministrations, and as such, didn't have its own Custodian division. Unless . . .

Hope resuscitated in his chest. Didn't the Iconoclasts have members infiltrated within the Custodians? Maybe Niko was grasping at straws, seeing signs that didn't exist. Or maybe the Iconoclasts hadn't abandoned him after all.

The drone flitted away, absconding into the night.

Niko lowered his gaze and arm, and stepped away from the edge.

"That's it," Marshal Hall coaxed. "Come back, Niko. You'll be going home soon."

Niko cast one final look at Paxania Stadium and allowed himself to be led back inside.

CHAPTER 15

IMANI

IMANI WAS EXTRAORDINARILY LUCKY. THERE WAS no other way to describe it—Game after Game, she won every single one of them. They were practice Games, of course, with no stakes aside from bragging rights and cementing herself as a legitimate Player.

"What's your secret?" Aric asked Imani while they played a lazy round of Labyrinth. The sprawling game board took up the entire desk. Today was technically an off day, but Aric wanted to brush up his skills and Imani didn't mind spending a couple hours playing her favorite game. "Coach doesn't let just anyone walk onto the roster."

They were in Imani's assigned housing unit, a simple but sufficient room appropriate for the Antarctican Republic Battle Team's newest member. Newest *and* oldest. In fact, as far as Imani knew, she was the only person to become a Player as a second career. Which made sense, considering most—if not all—Players were selected from a young age.

Be Niko Vandes. Kit's instructions sat heavy in

her stomach. Words she'd taken to heart. So, here she was, following Vandes' footsteps yet feeling very lost all the same.

Imani rolled the octahedral die and added two dynamite pieces to the board. She tried to imbue Vandes' confidence as she passed the die back to Aric. "Well, I'm not just *anyone*."

"Right," Aric agreed. "You beat Niko Vandes at his own game."

That had been the only reason why the Antarctican Coach even entertained the notion of letting Imani join the team. It wasn't a free pass, of course. Imani still had to play several rounds of try out matches. But she'd been prepared. Over the past couple weeks, she'd memorized the rules for all eight of the sanctioned Battle Games and spent countless hours brainstorming strategies with Kit.

Still, no one was more surprised than Imani herself when she swept through a 5-game winning streak against the Antarctican team's novice Players. Even when she played against the more veteran team members, she won more often than not.

"You know how I beat him?" Imani asked, watching Aric cuss when he rolled the skull icon on the die, wiping out half of his medical supplies.

"You got him to underestimate you," Aric guessed.

"I got lucky. Just like how I got lucky winning the lottery to be a Custodian."

Aric pursed his lips and played a *Stop and Search* card to recover 25% of his supplies. "Yeah, but you're also *good* at playing. No way luck is carrying you through all this."

She shrugged and held out a palm, a silent ask for the die. "Just like how there are *good* people out there yet luck wasn't enough to save them from getting fogged."

The frown deepened on Aric's face. He was twenty-two, but his round cheeks, blue eyes, and honey curls made him seem younger. (Either that, or life hadn't kicked him in the shins yet. Innocence and naiveness were the secret elixir of youth.)

She rolled the die and stared down at the number 1. "Never mind, forget I said anything."

Aric drew a sharp inhale when he noticed the number she'd landed on. "C'mon, please don't bomb my path. I'll trade you my map if you spare me."

Raising an amused eyebrow, Imani double stacked her *Aerial Warfare* cards and shook her head at Aric's groan. "Bargaining with your opponent like that will earn you a penalty in a real Game."

Aric flopped back in the chair. "Just take the win."

"Thanks, I will." She grinned then froze when a new message popped onto her utility-band.

"Everything all right?" Aric asked when Imani continued staring at the notification.

"I don't know." She stood and pushed the chair in. "Coach just summoned me."

"You'll be representing the antarctican Republic in the upcoming Peacetime Games," Coach Wen said. "Since you haven't participated in an actual Battle Game, you'll be in the Class III division. Nonetheless, playing your first officiated game at the 30th Peacetime Games is certainly a memorable way to debut."

Imani nodded, still processing the news. It was just the two of them in the Coach's office, which was in the building directly beside the dormitory that housed the novice Players. A digital frame hung behind the holo-glass desk, photos of the Coach and various Players flickering through. Perhaps one day, Imani would find herself among those images.

Wen continued, "Coach Solene and I have decided your strength lies in Set."

"Not Labyrinth?" Imani asked.

"Another one of your stronger games," Wen agreed. "But we have someone else in mind for that already."

"Who?" As far as Imani was aware of, she was the best novice Labyrinth Player.

"Aric Siasi."

Imani sputtered, "I literally *just* beat him thirty minutes ago at that game. Plus, everyone knows Quan is the best novice Set Player, not me."

Coach Wen sighed and laced her fingers atop the desk between them. "Believe me, I see where you're coming from, but I don't make the final call."

"Can I make an appeal?"

"Afraid not. Your name's already submitted on the finalized roster. Now, if you were to become critically ill or have something else happen under extraordinary circumstances, your designated backup would play in your stead. However, you'd forfeit any bonuses, so I strongly recommend you hone your Set skills and put your best move forward."

"I see."

Be Niko Vandes. Imani tightened her jaw. Vandes was a famous Setmaster. It was no coincidence she'd been selected for this Game. This all stunk of the Icono-clast's meddling.

"The prizes for winning a Class III game aren't nearly as grand as those in the Class II and Championship leagues, but placing in the top three will still earn you significant perks," Coach Wen said. "For example, you'll get an extra week of vacation time and a 10,000 credit reward. Do you have any questions?"

Imani shook her head. Her heart thudded in the back of her throat. Never in her life had she imagined she would get the chance to visit Paxania Stadium—the ticket prices were exorbitant, not to mention the cost of lodging on the island itself. Now, she was going to be in the heart of it.

"Wonderful." Coach Wen beamed. "The team's flying out in two days. Your uniform will be delivered tomorrow and—"

"Wait, I have a request."

Wen motioned for Imani to go on.

"Can I have a visitor before I fly out?"

"YOU LOOK TIRED," IMANI COMMENTED TO KIT.

They scowled but didn't deny the statement. "I've been busy."

"Busy with what?"

"Preparations." Tension radiated through their posture, the plate of food before them untouched.

With only thirty minutes left before visiting hours closed, the lounge was empty save Imani, Kit, a security guard posted by the door, and two junior Players messing with a street racing game in the far corner. (That was a for-fun video game, not an actual Battle Game game.)

"I know there's something you want to say." Imani reached across the table and speared the rainbow carrot slices off their plate. "Spit it out. I've got a flight to catch in ten hours." She dropped her voice, the image of her reflection brooding back at her in the large glass window behind Kit. "Any updates on Vandes? I haven't heard anything since the arrest." Her stomach plummeted as she set the fork down with a clink, appetite fleeing like citizens running from Karlo. "He's not de—"

"He's alive." Kit rubbed their eyes then leaned back in the booth. "I got visual confirmation last week. He's being kept on Paxania Island, as suspected."

"Do you need me to access the building he's—"

"I'll take care of the extraction efforts. Just focus on your upcoming Game."

She studied them for several seconds, noting their darting glances and fiddling thumbs. "You're still not telling me what you *really* came here to say. C'mon, Kit, talk to me. I'm just as committed to this operation as you are. I'm on the national Battle Team, for crying out loud! What do you need me to do during my match?"

They shot her a sharp glance. "Who said anything about you doing something extracurricular during your Game?"

She sniffed and took a dainty bite of the carrot. "Please, I get assigned to play Set after you tell me to *be* Niko Vandes? Only takes a braincell and a half to figure out there's something up your sleeve." Seeing that they still hesitated with divulging information, she gave one final push. "We're so close to the finish line, don't hold back now. Have I ever given you reason to doubt?

What's with the sudden misgivings?"

"Getting you onto the Battle Team was easy," Kit murmured. "The next part will be much more difficult. More dangerous."

Imani stabbed another carrot and chewed angrily, annoyed they were still being coy. "I'm not afraid."

"Never said you were." They pushed their plate over to her side. "How much do you care about saving Vandes? More than your own life?"

She slowed her chewing and swallowed. "If you're thinking of bargaining with the Court to trade my life for his, it's not going to work. Vandes is immeasurably more valuable than I am."

"That wasn't my plan, and you didn't answer the original questions."

"First tell me what I'm supposed to do."

Kit sighed then finally relented. "You're supposed to cause a distraction while the extraction team breaks out Vandes."

She nodded. It was about as much as she suspected— where else better to incite a spectacle than at the Peace-time Games itself? "What type of distraction, exactly?"

"I'm not sure." They cracked a wry smile. "It's above my pay grade. All I know is during your Game, you need to play a particular Set pattern—the Serene Invasion, do you remember that?"

"It's an unusual pattern. There aren't many instances where it makes sense to employ it . . . though, I reckon that's why it was chosen. Less chance of it accidentally being played through the natural course of the game. I'll have to make a purposeful intent to execute it. Does it matter when I complete the pattern?"

Kit shook their head. "Pattern completion will trigger the distraction. Don't ask me how—that's also above my pay grade. Your scheduled game time and location has already been published, so we know the window we're working with."

"All right, aside from playing the Silent Invasion, is there anything else I need to do?" She froze, the possibility of what came *after* finally hitting her in full force. Up until now, she'd been so focused on righting her wrongs she hadn't even considered what to do after Vandes was rescued. Was she expected to live the rest of her life as a Player? What if her ties to the Iconoclasts were exposed? Would the Iconoclasts offer her sanctuary?

She didn't realize she'd voiced her questions out loud until Kit answered, "Hopefully, if things go smoothly, Players and Battle Games will be remnants of the past. If the worst comes to fruition, we might be able to offer you limited protection."

A chime rang out from the speakers.

She stood and motioned for them to follow. "The lounge is closing in five minutes."

A darkness rolled across Kit's face. They sucked in a long breath and slowly released it, thumbs hooked in their jacket pockets. Their gaze flicked toward the ceiling before swooping down to meet hers. "This is me talking to you as a friend, not a . . . representative of the group. Okay?"

She raised a brow at their sudden change in demeanor. "Okay."

"Nobody's forcing you to do anything, Imani. Whether or not you trigger the distraction is up to you. If you do, great—we'll attempt the rescue. If not, nothing bad will happen to you. While the rescue would be called off and you'll lose the group's trust, no retaliation would be made against you."

Imani tilted her head, studying their solemn posture. "Why does it almost sound like you *don't* want me to go through with the plan?"

They chewed on their lower lip for a few seconds then released it with a huff. "I don't know, call it a gut feeling. The higher ups have been planning something big for this Peacetime Game. Obviously, plans have been modified since freeing Vandes is now a priority. But I can't shake the feeling I'm being purposefully kept in the dark because of my ties to you, and they're worried I might refuse to pass along your orders if I knew the full details."

She offered a soothing smile, both for their sake and her own, to quell the rising unease in her stomach. "Thanks for the warning, I'll be sure to keep that in mind."

They raked a hand through their thick, unruly hair, a nervous gesture. "Ah, hopefully I didn't screw up Vandes' fate by telling you that."

The laugh that burst out of her was stiff and tight. "I think we're both stressed and paranoid."

"Yeah, we're probably making monsters out of shadows." They nodded down at the half-eaten carrots. "How's the food here?"

She pulled a face, and they headed for the door. "Good enough, I suppose."

"That bad, huh?"

She groaned as they stepped out into the crisp evening. The Antarctican Republic's glacier-inspired architecture threw iridescent beams of light across the courtyard. Thick slabs of polarized glass served as the windows, walls, and doors of many buildings. Ocean-blue reinforcement joints provided a stark contrast at the edges and corners of the glass panels. A smile ghosted across Imani. Being surrounded by traditional building designs was one of the perks she'd genuinely enjoyed since moving onto the campus.

"Well." Kit shuffled their feet. "I guess I'll see you on the other side."

"See you." Imani watched them jog toward the bus stop by the main gate, then returned to her apartment unit.

She had a plane to catch, a Game to win, and revolution to aid.

CHAPTER 16

IMANI

PAXANIA STADIUM.

Not even Imani's wildest imagination could've conceived the sheer scale of the arena, the watchful pressure from the spectators, and the crushing noise surrounding her. And she wasn't even on the main stage.

The top Players battled it out on the central gaming platform raised a dozen meters into the air, while the novice and backup Players graced the perimeters on smaller stages. Half of the screens displayed continuous footage of the Championship League Games while the other half cycled through the secondary Games happening simultaneously.

Imani perused the Set board before her, a surveyor getting the lay of the land. Fifteen minutes in and she knew the win sat in her hand. While her opponent—a young man from the Central American Alliance—contemplated his next move, Imani surreptitiously scanned the crowd. She snorted and crossed her arms, redirecting her focus back onto the board. The Iconoclasts have been operating for decades and had mastered the art of camouflage. She wasn't going to spot Iconoclast agents. No, she should concentrate on winning this Game and playing the trigger pattern.

The other Player placed his stone, expression impassive as the timer light illuminated on Imani's side, indicating her 1-minute turn had begun. She plunked her stone down, setting herself up to surround her opponent's territory within three moves. The corner of his mouth twitched into a grimace as it was his turn to make a move once more.

Imani turned a stone over in her hand. It didn't feel any different from a regulation issued game piece, and nothing about the board stood out either. Not for the first time, she wondered how exactly the trigger would work. Was somebody watching her every move, waiting for her to execute the pattern and give the signal? But why have *her* give the signal?

A hundred questions whirled through her mind. Her leg bounced with nerves. She closed her eyes and exhaled. *Trust the process.*

"You going?" Her opponent's snide tone startled Imani, and the heel of her boot kicked into the table base, sending a needling burst of pain up her leg.

"Yeah, yeah." She scanned the board and was about to place her next stone to seal off his escape route, then paused.

If she did that, then she wouldn't have enough space to set up the Serene Invasion. Frowning, she searched for another way to block off her opponent until the timer sounded the ten second warning. Ah, screw it. She placed her stone in a spot that would at least let her start the pattern.

Predictably, the other Player seized the opening to escape the trap Imani had implemented. Her jaw tightened as she analyzed her remaining options. It wasn't looking good. The Serene Invasion required a lot of space, and the board was getting crowded. She had to claim the available spaces required for the pattern before her opponent took them—but that left her vulnerable to attacks.

Which was the crux of it all, wasn't it? The Serene Invasion wasn't often played because rarely was there a time when it made sense to use it. *Sometimes you've got to lose something to win something.*

She glared at the board and clenched the black stone in her fist. Lose the game to win Niko's freedom, that was the deal. Ignoring her instincts screaming to counter her opponent's move and regain footing on the board, she placed the second stone for the five-move pattern.

Imani gritted her teeth, watching the other Player's brows raise before making his next move and sweeping away several of Imani's stones to be replaced with his own. Apparently she had a competitive streak, as the idea of losing—even if on purpose—left a sour taste on her tongue and a bitter scent in her nose.

Wait.

She sniffed and tensed, dread prickling her scalp. She recognized the bitter-sweet scent, like burnt caramel. The scent was faint, but instead of fading away as Imani was accustomed to, she swore it was intensifying. She glanced under the table right as a breeze blew through, fanning that familiar scent into Imani's face.

She recoiled and stared at the small seam in the table base that must've accidentally split open partially when her boot banged into it. There. When she squinted at the right angle, unmistakable pink wisps slipped out the cracks before the wind whisked it away.

Karlo was here. Underneath the table.

A gasp caught in the back of Imani's throat as reality sank its claws into her. Of course she'd suspected that her life would be in danger by carrying out the Iconoclast's plan; Kit had made that abundantly clear. But she didn't think it was a *death sentence.*

Because there was no escaping Karlo, not without protective gear—and a whole damned *canister* of the killing fog was literally at her feet. She tucked away a grim smile. How fitting was it for Karlo to play both a pivotal role in her life and death.

She pressed the sole of her boot against the tiny seam, preventing the pink fog from slithering out. The Set board must be linked to whatever contraption the Iconoclasts had rigged within this gaming platform, and the Serene Invasion pattern was the code to set it into motion.

Niko Vandes, you are one lucky bastard. If Imani hadn't interfered, then it would've been Niko facing down Karlo. Did he know what he was getting himself into when he joined the Iconoclasts? Was he so willing to sacrifice his life for a cause? No doubt the widely broadcasted death of a famous Player would've been an absolute showstopper, a spectacle to set the stage for whatever other hijinks the Iconoclasts had planned to capitalize on Niko's untimely death.

But she was *Imani Tenzing.* In the celebrity pool,

she was a small fish where Niko was a whale. Which was probably why her life was only worth a distraction, a temporary diversion to rescue Niko.

"Do you even care about this game?" The other Player grumbled, then scoffed when Imani put down the next stone to complete the Set pattern.

A stupid move, for sure, that pretty much sealed off her fate.

He shook his head and continued sweeping her pieces off the board. "I don't know what tactic you're trying, but it's not working."

"Yeah, well, I don't know what I'm doing either." Imani placed the penultimate stone.

"Seriously? You're not even trying anymore."

By now, the gamecasters had finally noticed the unusual exchange happening on their platform. The cycling reels paused on their game while the gamecasters' confused commentary speculated what could be going on. Imani winced when the camera cut to Coach Wen's angry gesticulation. She tore her gaze away from the screen and studied the VIP booth instead. Members of the International Conflict Resolution Court sat in those premier seats, alongside the world's top leaders and most influential business mongers. They were too far away for Imani to discern their expressions, but she could *feel* the disapproval radiating off them as they turned to watch her. She could practically hear them hissing, *How dare you make a mockery of this Game? You don't belong here. You are a fraud.*

The timer dinged. Her turn. She rolled the ebony stone between her thumb and finger. Paused when she realized not only had the air taken on that familiar bitter-sweet scent, but now there was a texture, too. She rubbed her left fingertips together. Her finger pads came away slightly tacky, like she'd grabbed onto a handful of spun sugar and let it melt into her skin.

Fuck.

Smelling and seeing Karlo wasn't *good* per se, but it wasn't necessarily lethal. Feeling it, though, meant its concentration was approaching a dangerous limit.

Where *was* Karlo coming from? There had to be another source aside from beneath her table. Her spine stiffened. She swept her gaze across the massive fan blades pushing steady breezes across the crowd. All it took was one well-placed canister of Karlo and countless spectators would be dead within minutes.

Nobody else in the stadium had noticed Karlo's silent encroachment. How could they? Only a Custodian would recognize these warnings.

Beep beep beep. The ten second warning rang out, causing her heart to pulse in the back of her throat. Shit, how was time flying by so quickly? She chewed the inside of her cheek and studied the stone in her palm, the weight of its potential heavy and foreboding. It had been an easy choice when it was only her life at stake. But now it wasn't just her life, or a couple dozen lives—but *thousands* of lives.

Her eyes hooked onto the VIP booth. She knew with absolute conviction—the same way she knew objects fell and water wetted things—that she was not the Iconoclast's primary target. She was Imani Tenzing, small fish in the big fucking sea. She was a small fish—and small fish made perfect bait to sink this corrupt system.

What better time to shake up the norm than when

the norm was already destabilized? Wiping out the VIP booth gave the Iconoclasts the chance to replace those people with ones of their choosing, and from there, they could slowly cleanse and mend the International Conflict Resolution Court from the inside out.

At least that's what Imani hoped would happen.

Beepbeepbeep.

She smiled at the cam-drone flitting overhead and completed the Serene Invasion. Moments later, the unmistakable pink fog began to flood the stadium.

CHAPTER 17
NIKO

NIKO GAPED AT THE UNBELIEVABLE SCENE unfolding below.

Pink. Pink. Pink.

Karlo had found them. And somehow, Imani was the reason why. His head throbbed, brain whirling from the whiplash of the past six hours—being yanked out of his cell and brought to Paxania Stadium—*Welcome home,* Hall's words—seeing Imani, the last person he expected, playing in the Games—and now Karlo sweeping down the stands and pooling into the arena in an unstoppable tsunami, putting everyone into a peaceful, infinite slumber.

A Serene Invasion.

A bout of vertigo overcame Niko, and he took a step away from the tinted window overlooking the arena. He was locked in the highest spire of the thirteen peaks adorning the crown-shaped stadium. Like that stupid princess locked in the tower from an old world fairy tale, waiting for a hero to swoop in and save the day. Except instead of a knight in shining armor, it was Karlo swathed in pink.

His assigned guards muttered to each other and grunted into their comms. One walked to the door but didn't open it.

"So, what's the verdict?" Niko tilted his head toward the window. It was a thirty meter drop to the closest ground outside. "We've got some time before Karlo becomes a problem for us, but that doesn't mean we're safe yet."

Their height, in addition to being indoors, offered decent protection. Unlike the drones used to release Karlo at higher altitudes, whoever released the fog had started from the top of the bleachers. The heavy gas rushed down the stands like blood-tinged whitewater. The spires were safe . . . for now.

"What grade sealant do you think this room has?" Niko continued. "Grade 500? 600? Grade 900 and above should filter out most of the toxins, but unless the spire is its own closed system, the fog will eventually seep in."

"Shut up," Guard 1 grumbled. "We're standing by until we receive further orders."

Niko widened his eyes. "This seems like an emergency situation where you should've immediately received—oh, comms are down, aren't they?"

"I said to—"

The door shuddered with pounding from the other side, cutting off Guard 1.

"Marshal Hall has an evac drone on the way," a muffled voice called. "We're supposed to meet them at the lower balcony."

Guard 2 yanked on the door handle to let in the newcomer. He'd barely taken half a step before he collapsed with a sickening *thud*. Guard 1 jumped to the side, hand reaching for his gun. But the third person—Guard 3—strode in and jabbed something to Guard 1's neck before his hand even closed around the weapon.

Niko stared at the masked figure. They wore the standard guard uniform in addition to a respirator. Then Niko raised his hands in surrender because that seemed like the smart thing to do.

"I'm on your side." Guard 3 motioned for Niko to follow them out into the hall. "Name's Kit."

Niko stayed put and aimed a pointed glance at the two fallen guards.

"They're just asleep," Kit assured. "Like, actually asleep and not a euphemism for dead."

Niko lowered his arms but didn't budge from his spot by the window. "Won't they die if we leave them?"

Kit see-sawed their gloved hand. "Maybe, maybe not. Let's leave their fates up to chance."

"That feels wrong."

"Nah, we're just being karma's arbiter."

When Niko still refused to move, Kit made an impatient sound in the back of their throat and stepped deeper into the small room. "Let's *go*. I'm with the Iconoclasts. Do you know how much effort went into this rescue?" Their voice lowered, turned pleading. "Don't make Imani's sacrifice be in vain. She regretted what she did, you know. Felt horrible about turning you in and getting Aiden killed."

Niko flinched, the thought of Aiden reopening that cut in his chest. Staring back outside the window, the gaming platforms were completely obscured by a sea of pink fog. "We need to get Imani out of there."

Kit winced but shook their head. "No time. Come on, there actually is an evac drone waiting for us on the lower balcony. Put this on." They tossed him a respirator and mask. "We'll do a proper detox once we're on base, but this should get you out—hey! Where are you going?"

Niko ignored Kit's harried yelling as he tugged the respirator straps behind his head and dodged outside. The hall had been cleared, with two workers unconscious on the ground, no doubt thanks to Kit. He needed to get down to the lower levels. Since the spires were usually occupied by special guests, each had an elevator that linked to the underground tunnels leading out to the stadium's center, offering a discreet way to bypass the crowds and access the Players before a Game for meet and greets.

Niko swore when he reached the elevator, discovering it was out of service. The emergency alarms must've disabled it. He spun and beelined for the stairs.

"Niko!" Kit caught up and yanked on his shoulder. "If you go down, you'll get caught. It's swarming with guards."

"Who are probably too busy panicking over their own lives to notice me."

"Imani's gone." Pain lanced through Kit's voice, and their fingers dug deeper into Niko's flesh. "You're only endangering yourself—"

Niko pulled out of Kit's grip and charged down the stairs. "She might be alive. She's a Custodian—she knows how to maximize her chances of surviving."

Kit followed with a curse. Their boots pounding against the self-healing cement stairs echoed. "Look,

I know we like to believe *all lives are equal*—which is true—but at this moment, your life is *much* more impactful than Imani's. The Iconoclasts don't send in an extraction effort of this scale for just anybody."

A strangled laugh pushed out of Niko. His lungs burned and muscles ached, weaker than normal due to his lockup stint. "For real? Because I seem to recall having to fight my way into even being *considered* a potential member because I was a liability. So what gives?"

"We finally recognized your potential."

Niko shot a glare over his shoulder. "I want the real reason, not the palatable one."

"The memory chip with the Karlo recipe is passcode locked. We need you to unlock it."

"How did you get ahold of—ah, Imani gave it to you, didn't she? Anyway, why would *I* know the passcode?"

"Because it's Aiden's chip."

"The code is his birthday."

"We tried that already."

"His real birthday. 02032108." Niko jumped the last three steps on the landing, swung around the corner, then started down the next flight. "There. You have the info you want, you're free to go."

Kit paused and appeared on the verge of high tailing it back up to the balcony for a quick escape. But then they tipped back their head, groaned, and sprinted after Niko.

Together, they descended the stairs, taking two steps at a time. Of the few guards and stadium staff they encountered, no one paid them any attention, though, all too focused on climbing out of Karlo's reach. By the time they hit the bottom, the floor was completely deserted.

Niko wrinkled his nose. "Does it smell like burnt sugar?"

Kit jogged over to the door that led to the tunnels connecting the spire to the arena grounds. "That's the fog you're smelling. It'll get worse the moment I open this door. Keep calm but move quickly. Grab onto my shoulder so we don't lose each other. Your respirator isn't rated for this level of contamination so I have no idea how long it'll last. Our evac drone has a beacon on my location, so they're ready to pull us out at any moment."

They flung open the door and sped through the long tunnel. Red emergency glow strips pulsed along the top and bottom of the corridor, lighting curated moss-covered walls in distorted shadows. The bittersweet scent strengthened the longer they walked, and soon, curls of rose-colored mist snaked along the cement ground. A pack of rats skittered out from the darkness, startling Niko.

Kit huffed a laugh. "Easy, there. We'll see more creatures flushed out."

As it turned out, the second creature they saw was a human. One of the stadium groundkeepers lying prone in the middle of the hall. Kit barely spared her a glance before declaring, "She's gone."

Niko gulped and tightened his grip on Kit's shoulder as they marched forward. Pink fog swirled around them at waist height like they were wading through a sunset. "This is wrong. You can't murder thousands of people for one rescue mission."

Even though Niko couldn't see Kit's face behind the visor, he *felt* them roll their eyes. "A, don't beat yourself up over this. You didn't choose to release the fog, so none of this is your fault. B, don't flatter yourself into thinking you're the sole reason for this effort. Rescuing you, taking out the International Conflict Resolution Court members, and making a public statement were all motivation."

Niko nearly ran into Kit's back when they halted abruptly. Kit cautioned, "Brace yourself."

With that, they opened the second set of doors leading into the arena proper.

Niko gasped. A wall of pink clouds greeted them, so thick and widespread it was impossible to see anything else. Then, as if releasing a huge breath, the fog rushed in like a tidal wave. Niko's respirator whirred overtime, struggling to filter out the toxins. His exposed skin—face, neck, hands—prickled with numbing warmth. Although Karlo was only lethal if a large enough dose was inhaled, skin contact still left undesirable effects. Namely, loss of sensation. *Like falling asleep, my ass. More like sleep paralysis.*

Despite the mask protecting the worst of Karlo from Niko, his eyes and nose still burned. It was impossible to orient himself now that they were in the thick of the miasma. Off in the distance, he thought he could hear klaxons blaring and emergency vehicles flying overhead.

Kit grunted a warning but the blood roaring through Niko's ears drowned out the words. His feet tripped over something—definitely a body—and he stumbled into the Iconoclast agent. Kit's hand shot out to steady him. "Imani's platform is ten meters straight ahead."

"How can you see anything in this?" Niko could barely see past an arm's length.

"Infrared goggles. We'll need to climb up to fetch her. Luckily, they lowered the platform when the emergency alarm was triggered so we won't need a grapple. How are you holding up?"

"Good enough," Niko replied.

Kit chuckled without mirth. "I suppose that'll do for now. Here, can you pull yourself up?"

They moved Niko's arm off their shoulder and placed it on the edge of something cold and firm. Niko grabbed the platform and, with a jump, hoisted himself up. Kit quickly followed and guided Niko away from the edge.

"Can't be losing you right after finding you," they commented.

Niko squinted. He took a step toward the silhouette slumped in a chair. "That's her."

Together, he and Kit approached the figure. Pink swirled around her head like a halo when Kit waved their hand to clear the air. She'd fallen asleep with her head tipped back, staring up at the skies, hands neatly laced on her lap.

"I'll call in the drone," Kit murmured.

Imani's eyes were wide open, staring up into nothingness. No furrows wrinkled her cynical face. Instead, her mouth was a relaxed line, the tiniest upward curve at the corners. Almost like she was happy . . . no, that wasn't the right word . . . *content* for once. Not a superficial contentment, but the type brought on by inner peace and fulfillment.

Niko pressed his fingers against her pulse points but felt nothing. He shoved down despair, reminding himself that his extremities were numb from Karlo.

A sudden gust kicked in, momentarily dispersing the dense agglomeration of the fog. Niko glanced up and immediately wished he could erase the sea of unmoving bodies from his memory. The stadium aisles were clogged with attendees rushing for exits, Players still at their gaming platforms, and the VIP booth filled with security guards trying to evacuate their clients in vain.

"We targeted the Court members," Kit said darkly. "Made sure they wouldn't have the chance to flee on their private escape vehicles. They're the smudges on the tabula rasa needed to start anew. Speaking of escape vehicles . . ."

A shadow swept in from above and the distinct shape of a quadcopter hovered. Pink mist swirled and danced beneath the rotor outwash. Slivers of bright cobalt peeked in between the parted fog, a promise of blue skies ahead, once passed through the toxic storm.

"You first," Kit insisted when the tether dropped down. "I'll be right after with Imani."

"Promise?" Niko reached out to slide her eyes shut.

For once, it wasn't Niko bearing the weight of the world. For once, he wasn't responsible for the lives of whole populations. For once, it was Imani who played the game of Life or Death, and she'd paid dearly for it.

"Promise." Kit offered a sad smile. "She's a good friend of mine, too."

The next thirty seconds passed in a blur. Kit clipped Niko into the harness. The rope was winched up and a stranger with long red hair and tawny eyes behind her transparent face mask helped unbuckle Niko before sending the rescue line back down.

"Sit." The woman pointed at one of the free seats then turned to help Kit onboard. Her eyes widened as Kit rolled Imani's limp body into the middle of the cramped space. "Who's this?"

"A friend," Kit replied.

An icon, Niko thought.

The side door slid shut and the pilot from the cockpit informed, "Starting cabin decontamination, you should be good to remove haz gear in a minute."

Kit pushed back the hood of their jacket, revealing wavy hair. They nodded at the woman. "Thanks, Astrid. I owe you one."

"What possessed you to divert from the plan?" Astrid hissed, surefooted despite the vehicle's swaying motion. "You put the entire team at risk!"

Niko watched them haul Imani into the back chair as he struggled to clip his seatbelt with numb fingers. Did her eyelids flutter? Did she inhale oh so slightly? Or was it all wishful thinking?

Kit tightened Imani's seatbelt then collapsed into the chair beside Niko. They noticed he was still struggling with his buckle and reached over to help before clipping themself in place. "If we hadn't gone back for Imani, we would've lost this one." They nodded at Niko.

Astrid dropped into one of the seats facing Niko's row. "Huh. So you're the newbie everyone's making a fuss about. Hope you're worth the trouble."

Niko drudged up a weary smile, exhaustion catching up like a hammer blow. "Me too."

"Cabin clear," the pilot updated. "A route out of the airspace has also been identified. Brace for acceleration."

Niko shucked off his mask and sucked in a lungful

of fresh air. His clothes smelled faintly bittersweet. He passed the respirator over to Kit. "Thanks for letting me borrow it."

They'd removed their visor, revealing warm hazel eyes and a gentle expression. Kit took the equipment, stowing it into a duffle bag beneath the seat along with their own gear.

"Where are we going?" Niko asked.

"Home base, headquarters, whatever you want to call it."

"The submersible platform?"

Kit's eyebrows jumped up. "Aiden's told you about it already."

"Yeah. Said we would get sushi . . ." He winced at the sudden tightness in his throat.

"We can still do that, if you want."

Niko nodded slowly. "Yeah, that would be nice. Thank you."

He shifted in the seat, straightening to look out the tinted window. Far below, the topmost spires of Paxania Stadium jutted out from the sea of fog. Desperate fingers of a drowning man reaching for salvation. But up above, the sky shone blue, clouds filtering sunlight into a gilded haze as the pilot aimed the vehicle west.

"It's my favorite time," Kit said quietly. "Golden hour, when the end of the day is around the corner and the world is softened with the aura of possibilities that lie in tomorrow."

Niko looked back at them. "Golden hour, the time of changeover from day to night, from the old to the new."

"Exactly. You get it." They chuckled under their breath. "Of course you do, you're one of us."

One of us. The words clicked in Niko's chest like lock tumblers clicking into place. This was where he was meant to be. Not out on the gaming platform playing for an audience, but *here,* out of the spotlight and working for a brighter future.

The quadcopter banked, and Paxania Stadium fell out of view.

"May I never see that arena again," Niko said.

"May it never host another Battle Game again," Kit agreed strongly, then met Niko's gaze. "Welcome to the revolution."

EPILOGUE
NIKO

THE PLAYING CARDS WATERFALLED FROM Niko's fingers in a satisfying swoosh. Warm jazz music hummed in the earbud tucked into his left ear as he spun half the deck in his palm before deftly flicking out the top card and weaving it in and out of his fingers. The salt-tinged breeze ruffled his hair as he stood near the stern of the Iconoclast's headquarters in the middle of the Pacific Ocean. The gentle slaps of the waves hitting the sides of the submersible platform was barely audible this high up.

Though *platform* didn't quite encapsulate the nature of the Iconoclast's home base. The *Icon* was more stealth ship than platform—if stealth ships were over three-hundred meters long and a dozen stories tall, capable of submersing a kilometer underwater for weeks on end, and traveling at speeds over sixty knots.

"Whoa, you learning new tricks?" Kit's bright voice sounded from behind, instantly lifting Niko's mood.

They jogged over and set down the satchel slung across their shoulder. "I thought you were just learning how to shuffle again."

Niko twirled a card between two fingers. "Originally, yes, but then I decided to try for something more. The doctor says it'll help improve my mobility for these."

He wiggled his truncated fingers. The skin had healed over the raw wounds, though it still occasionally pulled uncomfortably from time to time. Kind of like his memories of Aiden. The shrapnel of Aiden's death had finally dislodged from Niko's ribs, the hurt clotted and scabbed over, leaving behind a fresh scar telling a story of survival.

"I'm leaving after the funeral," Kit said. "Got a board meeting to infiltrate."

He tucked the cards into a pocket. "Be careful out there. If they catch the slightest hint you're with the Iconoclasts . . . Everyone's been jumpy since what happened at the Peacetime Games."

As it turned out, breaking a cycle was *hard*. Sometimes it took one, two, three smashes before cracks started showing. Despite 90% of the International Conflict Resolution Court members perishing under Karlo, a second Court of substitutes had quickly been cobbled together.

But it was okay—good, even—that they hadn't completely shattered the International Conflict Resolution Court. When things shattered, you're left with a mess. But when things cracked, you have the chance to mend it to *your* liking. Have something crack enough times, mend something enough times, change something enough times, and you'll end up with something entirely different from the original without the mess.

"Don't worry, there's like, eight other Iconoclast agents seated on the Court who can help me out in a sticky situation." They grinned. "Plus, nobody ever suspects the janitor. Anyway, when are they putting you to work?"

Even now, Niko still marveled over the freedom the Iconoclasts had granted him, in no small part thanks to Kit.

What's the point of bringing Niko onboard if you're going to shackle his potential? Kit had argued to the team leads. *And no, he's not a risk. He knows betraying this organization isn't worth the consequences.*

They'd said the last sentence so casually and without malice, it'd been clear they weren't trying to threaten Niko, but rather simply state the truth of the matter with no ulterior motive. And that had been . . . nice.

Countless others would've taken advantage of Niko's situation and leveraged his vulnerabilities. Aiden would've sweet-talked Niko into believing this was the fairytale ending he wanted—the revolution, the companionship, the happily-ever-after, and surely Niko wouldn't be the villain ruining everything by not complying. Ivonna would've plied Niko with guilt, reminding him of the sacrifices made to get him into the Iconoclasts and pressuring him to see the revolution through. Both Aiden and Ivonna cared for Niko, to be sure, but only the version of him they wanted to see and could control.

But Kit was different. Instead, they'd advocated for Niko's independence.

Why are you helping me? Niko had later asked.

They'd winked. *Because Imani believed in you, and so do I.*

"I'm leaving tomorrow," Niko said. "Leadership wants to take advantage of the public's renewed hatred toward Karlo. Astrid's leading a team to hijack some networks for me to make a broadcast."

A pause of indeterminable length had been placed on all Battle Games. With the public wary of attending Games and the government clueless as to how the Iconoclasts had obtained vast amounts of the pink fog, Paxania Stadium had been silent as a grave. Not to mention, the public no longer trusted the government to keep them safe from Karlo, and with that mistrust came distance—and with distance came clarity. Unhappiness with the Battle Game system was at an all-time high, with protests and demands for restructuring the International Conflict Resolution Court stronger than ever.

"We're also picking up supplies for the antidote developments before returning to the *Icon*," Niko added.

Excitement danced across their hazel eyes. "You think the researchers are getting close?"

"Closer than ever. Imagine that, a world where Karlo no longer works. Now that would be radical."

A chime rang out from Niko's utility-band. He sighed and silenced the reminder. "Ready to head over for the service?"

Kit picked up the satchel and followed him down to the lower deck. "I wish you could've gotten to know Imani better. She's pretty awesome, aside from the whole getting-you-arrested part."

He laughed quietly. "From my brief impression,

she was a force to be reckoned with. Bravest person I've ever met."

"Because she wasn't afraid to play a game against you? Or because she sacrificed herself for the greater cause?"

"Because she had the courage to shift her perspective. Not many people have the strength to change their world views, and even fewer to act upon it afterward."

"Since when did you get so wise?" Kit elbowed him in the ribs.

"Wise, me? I don't know what I'm doing half the time."

"Staying alive?"

"I don't even know what I *want* most of the time."

Kit's gaze softened. "It's okay to not always know where you're going—there's no end game in life. Take time to figure yourself out, then do what feels right to you."

Kit's words wrapped around Niko's shoulders, soft and strong. *Do what feels right to you.* In those six words, they'd offered Niko the freedom of choice, permission to allow himself to *be.*

The mood quickly sobered when Kit removed the small wooden urn from the satchel as they approached the deck overhang.

Kit caught him staring and held the container out in a silent offer.

Niko shook his head, opting for the flowers and plants neatly laid out on the table. "She was your friend. You should do the honors."

He surveyed the selection: bundles of bamboo, wreaths of bay leaf, strings of black-eyed Susans, bunches of poppies. What the hells—he grabbed one of each then joined the small congregation gathered at the deck. He stood off to the side while Kit took their place at the front.

The sun dipped low in the horizon, gilding the swells and caressing everything with an aureate touch. Golden hour, when the promise of a new day and new possibilities hung in the air. The fresh scent of flowers mingled with the ocean salt.

Kit's melodious voice rose and fell with the waves. They didn't speak for long—which, somehow, Niko thought was what Imani would've preferred. They painted her as stubborn but caring, unassuming but brave, humble yet willing to make sacrifices so that something *better* would have a fighting chance.

The urn was tossed overboard followed by the garlands and bouquets. The ocean quickly swallowed Imani, sinking her down for an eternal sleep. But the plants and flowers remained floating, splotches of bright colors in the infinite sea. Bursts of hope in the overwhelming vastness.

Niko's lips curved into a solemn smile as he sensed Kit stand beside him, also staring out into the sunset. He'd never been so alone in his life before—cut off from his teammates and coaches and adoring fans—yet nestled between the ocean and Kit, he'd never felt so at home or hopeful either. Because where there was hope, there was a future.

ACKNOWLEDGEMENTS

It takes a community to bring a book to life—and this certainly was the case with *One Last Game*. I am incredibly touched and thankful for all the support this story has received throughout its journey. Patrick, thank you for getting the heart of the story in *One Last Game* and taking a chance with this book. Karly, it's been quite the ride together all these years! Thank you for believing in my writing through the thick and thin—having you in my corner has been an absolute honor and privilege. Liz, your patience and sharp insight has elevated this story to levels I couldn't have imagined . . . and of course, thank you for reading the bajillion iterations of *One Last Game*.

To my beta reading/hype family, The Landing Pigeons (Francesca Tacchi, Andrea Tatjana, and Marco Frassetto), you guys are the best!!! Thank you for years of support and friendship—and of course, writerly feedback and pet pics and pigeon memes. To my many critique partners and beta readers (in no particular order) who have helped this novella shine: Thea, E. S. Hovgaard, Victoria, Samantha, Sofia Robleda, and Alice Chao.

Last but certainly not least, thank you to my family and partner—mom, dad, little sis, and Daniel—your love and support has been instrumental in supporting my writing.

ABOUT THE AUTHOR

T.A. CHAN is a human being trying to live her best life on this floating piece of space rock. She has a passion for fantasy and sci-fi books. During her free time, she's probably begging her plants not to die or spoiling the dog. She also has an unhealthy obsession with manatees, triangles, and dark chocolate. Her YA novel *The Celestial Seas* is forthcoming in 2026 from Viking. She is represented by Karly Dizon and Laurie McLean at Fuse Literary.

OTHER TITLES FROM FAIRWOOD PRESS

*Obviously I Love You
But If I Were a Bird*
by Patrick O'Leary
small paperback $11.00
ISBN: 978-1-958880-37-1

Space Trucker Jess
by Matthew Kressel
trade paper $20.95
ISBN: 978-1-958880-27-2

Shifter and Shadow
by Sharon Shinn
trade paper $16.99
ISBN: 978-1-958880-36-4

When Mothers Dream: Stories
by Brenda Cooper
trade paper $18.99
ISBN: 978-1-958880-35-7

*Better Dreams, Fallen Seeds
and Other Handfuls of Hope*
by Ken Scholes
paperback $19.99
ISBN: 978-1-958880-32-6

Changelog: Collected Fiction
by Rich Larson
trade paper $20.95
ISBN: 978-1-958880-33-3

Black Hole Heart and Other Stories
by K.A. Teryna
trade paper $18.99
ISBN: 978-1-958880-29-6

*A Catalog of Storms:
Collected Short Fiction*
by Fran Wilde
trade paper $18.99
ISBN: 978-1-958880-31-9

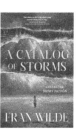